Harlequin

is pleased to announce the forthcoming release of its first motion picture, based on the best-selling novel by Anne Mather

Harlequin Presents...

KEIR DULLEA · SUSAN PENHALIGON

Leopard in the Snow

KENNETH MOR

featuring GORDO

and JEREMY

Produced by JOHN

Screenplay by ANNE MATHER

Directed by GERRY O'HARA

An Anglo-Canadian Co-Production

OTHER
Harlequin Romances
by DOROTHY CORK

Breakers on the Beach

by

DOROTHY CORK

Harlequin Books

TORONTO • LONDON • NEW YORK • AMSTERDAM • SYDNEY

Original hardcover edition published in 1977
by Mills & Boon Limited

ISBN 0-373-02115-1

Harlequin edition published November 1977

CHAPTER ONE

AFTER Berry Addison had left—and that was before lunch—there had been no callers at Overlooking, Eden's grandfather's small esoteric art gallery that stood on a low hill several miles out of Kamballa, a country town in northern New South Wales. Eden had had no company except that of the galahs which staggered about on the grass beyond the white gravel, looking for seed. They came there around five o'clock each day, which was now.

And now, by a curious coincidence, two cars were coming up the winding red drive from the road, their bonnets shimmering in the heat. The second car belonged to the King of Diamonds—Eden, who had been idly watering the garden, could see as she stood in the shade of the yellow box tree, watching. So he was back from the auction sales in Brisbane a day early, which meant either that he had got what he wanted or that there were no paintings there that interested him. The other car, the one in front, she did not know. It was certainly not Berry's moke, anyhow, though he had told Eden he might call in again later, and that was just as well. Because the King of Diamonds didn't like Berry.

He wasn't going to like the look of her much either, she suddenly realised, glancing down at her bare muddied feet and the rolled-up legs of a pair of jeans that had started off white but had somehow become more than slightly grubby as she pottered round the garden. Not the best of gear in which to welcome potential clients, she admitted, and she began to run rather guiltily towards the house, almost as if she could get there in time to change and present the

5

svelte appearance of the Pomeroy family, rather than the casual look of a Dare.

She was mincing gingerly across the white quartzite gravel just as the car in front pulled up and the driver—a male—leaned out to ask drawlingly, 'This is the Overlooking Gallery, I presume?'

'Yes.' Eden tried to look poised and all of her twenty years, though she had an idea she wasn't making much of a success of it. She thrust back a strand of hair from one cheek, then wondered too late if she'd left behind a smear of red mud.

'I hope your hasty formation of yourself into a reception committee isn't an indication that there's no one responsible around.'

Eden crimsoned and bit her lip. Cynical greenish-blue eyes assessed her disparagingly from beneath thick eyebrows, and a long expressive mouth was curved disparagingly as their owner emerged from the car and stood surveying her, hands on narrow hips that were encased in pale putty-coloured trousers.

'Mr Pomeroy,' said Eden coolly, 'is right on your tail.'

He turned his head and she took the opportunity to disappear, nipping smartly up the steps and through the front door; past the closed door of the gallery, and making a bee-line for the sanctuary of her bedroom. She shouldn't have spoken to a client like that, of course, but she had always had to watch her tongue. With fingers that shook slightly, she peeled off the pale coral top that had somehow got in the way of the hose, and stripped off her soiled jeans. She dragged a cotton dress from the wardrobe and pulled it over her head, sliding her feet into sandals as she did so. She reached for her hairbrush and used it hastily, and was at the door in time to hear the King of Diamonds bellow her name.

'Eden!'

'Coming, Grandfather!'

Now what? she wondered, making a face as she hastened to the gallery.

'Where,' demanded her grandfather as she appeared at the door, 'is the flower painting I was holding for Mr Watermount?'

Eden blinked, and looked quickly at the tall thirtyish man who stood with his back to the window. So that was Mr S-for-Sinclair Watermount. She had thought he would turn out to be either elderly and meticulous, or young and frightfully arty—ringing through to the Gallery so keen to get hold of a particular painting that had been featured in the advertisment in an antiques magazine. Instead, Mr Sinclair Watermount was thirtyish and very much a man of the world; striking though one would not say handsome. Tough —swaggering——

She jumped a little as her grandfather said thunderously, '*Well?*'

'Where you put it, I should think,' Eden said, and regretted at once that it sounded cheeky. She crossed to the big cherrywood chest in the large drawers of which her grandfather was accustomed to store paintings that were for one reason or another not to be displayed. It was already open and the King of Diamonds, who was now angrily twirling his curly silver moustache, had obviously already made a search. Eden saw in a few seconds that the picture was not there. Yet it had been there this morning—she had shown it, among others, to Berry.

'It's not there!' she exclaimed in surprise, and turning, found herself pinned securely between the accusing blue eyes of her grandfather and the coldly disturbing blue-green ones of Mr Watermount.

'No, it's not there,' agreed her grandfather. 'So why is it not there? You haven't by any chance, despite my strict and often-repeated instructions to you not to make any

7

sales whatsoever in my absence—you haven't sold it, I hope? Or otherwise disposed of it?' He flipped through the pages of the big accounts book with the barest of glances. 'There's no record here.'

'Of course I haven't, Grandfather. I—I just can't think what's happened to it, that's all.'

His lips twitched angrily and he stroked his silver beard. 'Who has called in my absence?' he rapped out.

Eden hesitated for a second. Berry could hardly be counted as a caller. He was her own personal friend.

'Nobody,' she said firmly, and knew that guilty colour had flooded her face. But Berry wouldn't have—oh, surely Berry *couldn't* have—— Even as the ghastly thought came into her mind, her gaze went to the window where, as if conjured up by some horrible magic, Berry's disreputable moke was pulling up behind Mr Watermount's lustrous blue vehicle. Her grandfather had of course put his car in the garage, so Berry was in blissful ignorance of the fact he was home again. She watched fascinated as he climbed out of the front seat, leaned into the back and produced something large and flat, wrapped in brown paper. He then came jauntily towards the house. Eden's heart did a dive and she closed her eyes unbelievingly for a second. What had he been up to?

Her mind flicked back uneasily to the morning—to the moment when she told Berry she couldn't even sell him a painting, let alone allow him to take something away on spec. Her grandfather would be apoplectic, she had said, and besides, the flower painting was very valuable—practically antique for Australia, and being specially reserved. Later, she had gone to the kitchen for cold drinks and to spread biscuits with the country paté she had made herself. Berry had been in the garden when she came back. And he must have commandeered the picture while she was away. 'Oh, the fool!' she thought in dismay. Now her grandfather was back a day early, and was Berry going to have some explaining to do! It was just as well he hadn't somehow managed to sell the thing.

She moved guiltily as the doorbell rang. 'It's Berry Addison, Grandfather. I'll get it.'

He cast her a cold and suspicious look and left the room himself. Eden drew a deep anguished breath and relaxed against the pale french grey wall. Berry would talk his way out of his predicament somehow. He had an agile mind as well as a lot of charm—not that his charm went over very big with the King of Diamonds. The sticky thing was that, in fact, her grandfather positively disliked him.

Contemplating her still muddy toes that peeped out of her sandals, Eden recalled the initial cause of that dislike. There was first of all, of course, the basic fact that her grandfather didn't encourage her to make friends in the town. Ever since she had come out to him from England about three months ago, he had expected her to devote all her energies to him and his interests—just as her Aunt Sylvia had presumably done. On this particular afternoon she had cycled in to town to bank the money, mostly cheques. There were art buffs at the gallery and her grandfather, who usually did the banking himself, couldn't get away. Before she got as far as the bank Eden had run into Berry by sheer chance, and had coffee with him, and by the time she got to the bank it was closed. So as not to incur the wrath of the King, she had told a white lie, meaning to slip into town the following morning and remedy her error, but for reasons of his own—or because he had a suspicious mind—he had rung through to the bank before she could get away and discovered her omission.

A positive inquisition had followed—led astray by a man, business forgotten, George Pomeroy and duty forgotten——

Eden raised her eyes and discovered that Sinclair Watermount, who she had thought was taking a look at the pictures on the gallery walls, was instead taking a long, hard, and definitely critical look at Eden Dare.

He watched her from under lowered brows, his broad-shouldered, narrow-hipped body utterly relaxed yet somehow suggesting to Eden a dormant strength—as if he could pounce if he wanted to and—and eat her. She felt, in fact, about as defenceless as a mouse, and as unimpressive in her immaturity. She was suddenly and uncomfortably aware of the jejune effect of her cotton dress, her dirty feet, her hastily brushed almost blonde hair pushed back behind her ears. She stared back at him, silently daring him to outstare her. He had a striking face, a broad square forehead that shadowed eyes that were more green than blue. His cheekbones were definite, his jaw jutting, and there were lines at either side of his rather wide mouth. Eden rather thought she was winning the staring competition, and then he disconcerted her by screwing up one eye, and she blinked, blushed and lost.

She turned her head as her grandfather came back into the room followed by Berry, who smiled confidently at Eden and raised one eyebrow in a way that she knew well. Relieved, she smiled back, her instant thought being, 'Everything's all right—he's talked his way out of it'. Though certainly her grandfather was looking far from affable, and the remark he shot at her rocked her composure entirely.

'So you've lied to me once again, Eden.' He stared at her for two seconds, then went to his big leather-topped desk, where he set down the now unwrapped picture that Berry had been carrying.

Eden looked at him indignantly, about to retort that she hadn't lied, then recalled that she had told him there'd been no callers. She shrugged and grimaced slightly. It was done now—but that little word 'again'! What sort of a

10

girl did that make her appear? Eyes smouldering, she glanced at Sinclair Watermount, whose expression was now one of cynical disparagement. Well, she couldn't be worried by what he thought of her, but she was thankful when he joined her grandfather across the room to take a look at the painting.

'Berry, how awful!' she whispered then. 'Why on earth did you do it? Thank goodness you brought it back, anyhow. But what did you tell Grandfather?'

He cocked an eyebrow and grimaced. 'I said you'd given me permission to borrow the thing, of course.'

'*What?*' Eden was dismayed. 'But I told you it was being specially kept for someone.'

'Oh, I know that—and of course he brought it up. So I said you must have forgotten.'

'You put all the blame on me—just like that?' she protested in an angry whisper. 'How could you?'

He shrugged and put a hand on her arm pleadingly. 'Now don't be thick, Eden. What else was I to say? You know the old boy—he'd have been quite likely to call in the police otherwise.'

'Of course he wouldn't,' she whispered. 'And anyhow, you shouldn't have taken it in the first place.'

'Oh, come off it, Eden, don't start preaching. If this guy had been interested enough, I could have made myself at least a couple of hundred bucks and still handed over your grandfather's asking price. It's not the sort of chance you pass up easily.'

Eden stared at him with hostility. This was a side of Berry, with whom she had thought herself more than a little in love, that she didn't know at all, and she moved away from his touch. 'It is if you're honest. And now what sort of spot do you think you've put *me* in?'

'Oh, you're all right—you're his granddaughter,' Berry said impatiently. 'Anyhow, you could have warned me he might be back today instead of saying it would be to-morrow.'

'Could I? I didn't see any need for warnings, even if I'd known. And nothing would have happened if you hadn't sneaked in behind my back and——'

'Stolen it?' He was angry now too. 'I've been honest—I've brought the thing back. In any case, it's done now. There's no sense in your being self-righteous about it. It'll all blow over in a day or two, so just forget it, can't you?'

As they whispered heatedly together, Eden was aware that the other two men were discussing the painting. Her grandfather was probably giving one of his scholarly-sounding dissertations on early Australian painting, because now they had moved across to stand looking at a picture showing a scene of the early gold-digging days. Eden ignored Berry. She felt bitterly hurt—her pride was hurt. She couldn't mean much to Berry if he could ride roughshod over her feelings like that! And he had certainly gone down in her estimation. It wasn't amusing to be made to look so sneaky and cheap, and a liar as well—with a stranger listening in too. And all to save his own skin. She was far from perfect herself, and admitted it, but she simply couldn't accept with equanimity the attitude he took ...

Her grandfather had now shifted his attention back to her and Berry, and Eden was conscious of her red cheeks. She clenched her teeth when Berry said smoothly,

'I hope everything's in order with the painting, Mr Pomeroy. I took care it wasn't damaged in any way. I'm really sorry about the misunderstanding. It was just a slip-up on Eden's part, that's all. It could happen to anyone. I hope you won't be too hard on her, sir.'

George Pomeroy listened unsmilingly and without interruption to his speech. He then advanced to the door and stood by it as he said frigidly, 'Eden was very well aware of the facts of the matter and of course she will be

12

punished. As for you, Mr Addison, this is the last time you and my granddaughter will whisper in corners behind my back. In future, you will do me the favour of keeping away from my gallery, my house, and my granddaughter. Good day to you.'

Berry's angled eyebrow rose higher. He made a little grimace, shrugged at Eden and left the room—and the house.

Eden stayed exactly where she was, writhing inwardly. She tried not to look at Sinclair Watermount as she wondered bitterly if her punishment would be pronounced immediately—and publicly—and what it was to be. Bed without tea? Bread and water for a week? Her grandfather looked as if he could mete out deserts as absurd as that, she thought, and was aware that her expression had become defiant, and that in Sinclair Watermount's eyes she must look like a naughty schoolgirl—unless he saw her as some kind of a delinquent.

She tossed her hair back and put up her head, and more to assert herself than for any other reason told Sinclair Watermount, 'I hope you're going to enjoy your picture, Mr Watermount, now you've got it safe and sound.'

'Thank you,' he said with a crooked smile and contempt still in his eyes. He added dryly, 'However, as it's a wedding present for my sister, I shall have the opportunity of enjoying it for only a few weeks.'

'Oh, I see,' Eden exclaimed impulsively. 'I couldn't imagine a painting of flowers driving you exactly wild. I'd have thought your tastes would run more to——'

She broke off as her grandfather snapped out, 'That's quite enough, Eden. Your opinion is of no interest. You may go.'

He didn't say 'To your room', but he might just as well have done so. The effect was the same, and it was all she could do to manage a jaunty smile before she disappeared.

13

She did go to her room, and stood forlornly at the window looking out at the straw-coloured countryside, where a few sheep strayed in the golden light of sunset. The tree shadows reached out long arms and a flock of galahs flew overhead, their undersides rose-coloured against the fading sky. Presently she heard the sound of a motor as Sinclair Watermount drove away, and she grimaced and thought, 'I shall never have to see *him* again, anyhow', a thought that proved later to be entirely wrong. She never wanted to see Berry Addison again either, as a matter of fact. She was through with him and thoroughly disillusioned.

It struck her forcibly that coming to Australia had been a complete and utter disaster. She was sure she would have liked her Aunt Sylvia, her mother's sister, but let's face it, she thought realistically, her grandfather didn't improve on acquaintance. He was as cold and arrogant and selfish as could be, and he didn't care a fig for her. She just couldn't go on living with him for much longer—she would have to break away and find some way of earning her own living, she mused, staring into a world that was rapidly darkening.

She didn't see her grandfather again until dinner time. She grilled steak and made a tasty tomato pie to go with it, then prepared a tossed salad, wondering the while what he would have to say about the happenings of the afternoon —and what punishment he had thought up for her.

But at dinner, he said exactly nothing, sitting opposite her at the round cedar table covered with a lacy écru cloth crocheted by Aunt Sylvia, at some time during a life spent apparently at the beck and call of her father. From the windows here one could see the glittering lights of Kamballa, and Eden fixed her attention on them and tried to ignore the fact that her grandfather was ignoring *her*. He was a handsome man, rather stocky, with bright blue eyes

14

and a ruddy complexion—and a curling silver beard and moustache that had caused her, when she first met him, to name him in her secret mind the King of Diamonds. She couldn't see in him any resemblance to her mother, who had been Valerie Pomeroy until, at twenty-one, she ran away and married Michael Dare, an Englishman. The old man, Eden realised now, had never forgiven her. He was voraciously possessive, and in his eyes she had deserted him.

In those days he had owned an antiques business in Brisbane and he had made a small fortune from it, but during the past few years his business had become more specialised, more in the nature of a glorified, though remunerative, hobby. He had moved to Kamballa with Sylvia, his only other offspring, and bought this old house, Overlooking, that had once been the homestead on a large sheep station. Eden had to admit that its rooms made a suitable background for his collection of paintings. Paintings were all he dealt in now, and he had a quite extraordinary ability to nose out unrecognised treasures from Australia's past. A discreet advertisement appeared now and again in an art or antiques magazine, and art collectors had no hesitation in travelling to this smallish town in northern New South Wales to run down what was to them rare treasure.

Eden had learned much of this from her mother, who had been kept up to date by letters from her sister, of whom she was very fond. 'Your grandfather is much too busy to write,' she had told Eden more than once, and so Eden didn't know that the old man had virtually banished her from his life until he told her himself.

When Eden's mother died after a long illness, Sylvia invited Eden to come and live with her. She was to pay her own fare—and now she knew why, guessing that Sylvia had been treated by her father much as Eden was treated now—rewarded for her work with no more than pocket money and her keep. Poor Sylvia had died suddenly only a few days before Eden left England. Eden knew nothing of this, and when she reached Kingsford Smith Airport there was no one to meet her. She was relieved when an announcement come over the public address system for Miss Eden Dare to call at the information desk. There was a message there from her grandfather, telling her to transfer to the domestic terminal where her flight was booked to a big town near Kamballa. She had just about an hour in Sydney, instead of the few days that her aunt had promised.

The news of her aunt's death when she was met by her grandfather came as a shock to her, and as it happened the whole aspect of her future life was changed. Instead of finding work in Kamballa as she had hoped to do, she was more or less incarcerated at Overlooking with an elderly man whom she found she could not learn to like even though he was her grandfather. She was expected, she discovered very quickly, to take up where her Aunt Sylvia had left off, and that meant in the main that she was to become a kind of unpaid housekeeper.

'You will have certain other responsibilities,' her grandfather had told her the day she arrived—after he had first outlined her main duties. 'I have never employed an outsider at Overlooking, and God willing I never shall—provided you can fill my daughter's place satisfactorily. Your mother, regrettably, was more Hart than Pomeroy. Your father I met only once.' He paused and frowned disapprovingly. 'We shall soon see what kind of stuff you're made of and how much Pomeroy blood flows in your veins. And if it's rich and strong you may expect to be rewarded accordingly.'

Well, it had not proved to be very rich and strong, Eden thought rather comically over dinner, looking across Aunt Sylvia's cloth at a grandfather to whom she was apparently invisible The Dare blood—or the Hart blood—appeared to be prevailing, and personally she was glad it was.

Dinner over—and if he had enjoyed it he didn't tell her so—he pushed back his chair and announced crisply, 'When you've done the dishes, Eden, you will come to the sitting room and we shall discuss your behaviour.'

'What behaviour?' she asked quickly. But he had turned away and didn't answer the question.

She wondered again as she did the dishes what her punishment was likely to be. She hoped he wouldn't go so far as to forbid her to go into town for the next month or anything like that. Her liking for Berry Addison's company had gone somewhat sour, but she did want to see Amy Blythe, the only other real friend she had made. Would there be any point in protesting her innocence again? She didn't really think so. Besides, it would be telling tales on Berry, and that sort of thing wasn't really in line with her ethics ...

In the sitting room, her grandfather sat by the reading lamp, smoking a cigar and reading an article in an art periodical. Eden stood waiting for his attention for several moments, but though he certainly knew she was there he didn't glance up, and suddenly she was exasperated. It was a long time since she had been a schoolgirl, and it was ridiculous that she should be treated like one now.

'Grandfather,' she said clearly, 'do you want to see me, or shall I go away?'

He set the magazine aside and looked at her with cold displeasure, from her sandalled feet to the top of her head and her now sleekly brushed and shining hair. Then he straightened the already stern line of his lips and began to pronounce judgement—and finally a sentence far more severe than she had imagined.

'I have given considerable and troubled thought to what occurred today, Eden. I have already been disappointed in you—lies, deceit, irresponsible behaviour ... you are not a Pomeroy, that much is very clear. It would appear that

17

you must take after your father. My life's work, my gallery, they mean nothing to you, and it would seem that there's little point in continuing our association. I don't ask for explanations, there can be none. But you've offered me no apology, you've been completely and unrepentantly defiant. Your moral standards would appear to be very low, which is perhaps not surprising when I consider your background.' He paused, and Eden bit hard on her lip to hold back an angry retort. He hadn't even known her father, and his slighting remarks made her blood boil.

'I know, of course, what the object of your exercise was,' her grandfather continued. 'I'm not a fool. I know very well that you and your friend planned to make a profit out of a painting that you had no right to sell.' Eden flushed deeply, because that was exactly what Berry had planned, and he observed it and smiled unpleasantly. 'Anyone who can engage in such practices has no place in my life. You will please pack your bags tonight, Eden, and leave my house in the morning.'

Eden's grey eyes widened. Did he really mean it? Or did he expect her to break down and beg for forgiveness—for mercy? She certainly wasn't going to do that. She would leave—it might be the best thing that had happened to her. She would go to Amy tomorrow. She would find work —she wasn't entirely useless. She had practically run the handicrafts shop at home ever since she left school because of her mother's failing health. She put her chin up.

'Very well, Grandfather. As you don't trust me, I shall go. I shall find a position in Kamballa. That was what I really intended to do when I came here.'

He was at least slightly disconcerted, and he gave her a sharp look before he said, 'You won't find it easy. You have few qualifications, if any, and no references. But I suppose in fact that you intend to run off with that fool Berry Addison. Just like your mother.' He reached for his read-

18

ing matter as if he had lost interest. 'It's unfortunate that you ever took it into your head to come out to visit me—a waste of time, a waste of money.'

'It was,' Eden agreed. She could have mentioned that she had not come out to *him*, and that the money to pay for the flight had been hers, but she didn't. As for running off with Berry Addison, that was about the last thing she would want to do. If his idea was to teach her a lesson, and if he thought she would come creeping back, with her head hanging, a sadder and wiser girl, then he was going to be disappointed. Eden Dare had a lot of pride—even if she wasn't a Pomeroy. And she would find work of some sort if it killed her.

She stopped and dutifully kissed her grandfather's unresponsive cheek.

'Goodnight, Grandfather,' she said cheerfully. 'I'll go and pack my things.'

He raised his head as she reached the door and said, 'If you have ideas of presenting yourself at the Art and Decoration shop in town, I warn you I shall not feel able to recommend you. Apart from your total irresponsibility, you know nothing of art or of objets d'art.'

'I shall make out,' she said airily, with a confidence that she didn't altogether feel. The thought of that particular shop had crossed her mind, and while her knowledge didn't amount to much, she had learned *some* things when she lived in England. She did have some discernment too— not that he would agree about that. He had actually told her once after a client had asked her opinion of a painting and she had given it, 'Don't think you've become an expert overnight because you can parrot off a few phrases you have heard me use. Whether *you* like a painting or not is irrelevant. If ever again you're asked such a question in my gallery, keep silent, smile, and look to me.'

'And say cheese,' Eden had thought wryly at the time.

Well, she would keep smiling and saying cheese she thought as, in her bedroom, she sorted and folded and packed her clothes, and gathered together her few belongings.

Lying in bed later, she began to think of the next day. It would be Sunday and Amy Blythe, who was a schoolteacher, was pretty sure to be at home. There was a spare bedroom in the apartment which belonged to Amy's parents; they were spending Mr Blythe's long service leave in Greece, so she wouldn't be a bother to anyone. She would be right in town—right on the spot—when it came to looking for work. And thank heavens, she still had a little money left.

It would be pleasant to stay with Amy, Eden reflected dreamily. She liked her very much. As for Berry, she would keep well away from the bookshop where he worked and hope she didn't run into him. She didn't want to see him again for a long, long time. She felt she had learned a somewhat salutary lesson from him. She had rushed into *that* friendship, believing ingenuously that his character matched the pleasant appearance he presented to the world. Her mental image of Berry's dark hair and good-looking face with the once fascinating crooked eyebrow was suddenly and disconcertingly supplanted by another image— the lean and cynical face of that older, hard-bitten type; Sinclair Watermount, who had been after the flower painting not for himself, but as a surely lavish wedding gift for his sister.

What type of a man was he? she wondered. Did his personality match his appearance? If it did, then she didn't think she would care to get mixed up with *him*. But she need hardly worry her head about that. Since she was leaving Overlooking, she would scarcely be likely ever to set eyes on him again ...

She was cheerful and matter-of-fact in the morning, and

if her grandfather had expected her to be red-eyed and downcast then he was mistaken. To tell the truth, by now she was actually looking forward to making the move and to becoming independent. She prepared breakfast and afterwards washed up as she always did. She put the last few odds and ends in her bag, then went into the gallery to ask if she might use the telephone to ring for a taxi.

Her grandfather didn't ask her where she would go, and Eden didn't offer to tell him. He probably didn't approve of Amy anyhow, because she would be, in his opinion, too pretty for a schoolteacher. But before she left the room, she hesitated and then asked him, 'Grandfather, who will cook your meals and do the shopping and keep the house tidy?'

In spite of everything it worried her, but there was a little gleam of triumph in her grandfather's eye as he told her dryly, and rather unfairly, 'You have never seemed particularly interested in my welfare, Eden. I hardly expected that would worry you. However, I have already arranged for old Mrs Cartwright's daughter from the poultry farm along the road to come and take care of my simple needs. She obliged me when my daughter was ill, and she's happy to do so again.'

'Then that's fine,' said Eden, and she meant it. 'I'll keep in touch, Grandpa. I'll let you know when I get a job.'

His silver eyebrows rose. 'That may well take longer than you think. I have no doubt at all that you'll be back, begging me to give you another trial. But——'

Eden looked him straight in the eye. 'But you won't, Grandfather? I'm altogether too bad a lot to expect mercy?'

He frowned and glared at her as if she were being altogether too insolent. Then the telephone rang and he answered it. He was still talking—art, of course—when her taxi came, and she went without him even seeing her go.

In Kamballa everything went as she had planned to

begin with. Amy was delighted to be able to put her up —delighted too that she had escaped from that 'fanatical old man', as she put it. Eden told her briefly and restrainedly about Berry's role in the affair, and Amy's reaction was that she had never felt that Berry was to be trusted—but he had helped Eden escape from Overlooking, so he had served some purpose.

However, her grandfather had been right when he said Eden would find it hard to get work. There just seemed to be nothing going for her in Kamballa, though she trudged the streets for the next two days, and assiduously studied the 'wanted' ads in the local paper. There was a handicrafts shop and it seemed reasonably busy, but the people who ran it, two sisters called Martin, assured her, though with polite regret, that they were able to handle it themselves. Amy, rather oddly, seemed quite philosophical about her failure to find work, almost as if it didn't matter to her very much if Eden didn't find a position.

It was December, the last week of the school term, and on Wednesday, unsuccessful again, Eden came back to the flat which was in a side street shaded by cedar trees and oleanders, feeling tired and dispirited and hot.

'No luck?' asked Amy, who was draped on the cool boards of the polished floor of the living room. She had changed into shorts and a bra top, and she was drinking iced orange drink from a long glass. She waved a hand in the direction of the glass jug on the coffee table. 'Help yourself, Eden—you look dried out.'

Eden felt dried out. She poured herself a drink and for the first time she could have cried. Amy had mentioned going over to the coast for the summer vacation, and when she had gone Eden would be on her own and, if she wasn't lucky, running out of cash. It wasn't a cheerful prospect.

She sat down at one end of the sofa and tried hard to

sound as if she wasn't worried. 'There aren't any jobs going for shop assistants in this town. I guess I'll have to look further afield.' She thought of her meagre savings. They wouldn't last long in one of the big cities while she job-hunted. 'Maybe I'll have to be a mother's help or something.'

'You will not!' Amy sat up and hugged her bare knees, her curly brown hair falling over her forehead. Her hazel eyes looked affectionately at Eden. 'You don't have to rush it, you know. The thing is, all the shops have already engaged extra staff for the Christmas rush. You'll have a better chance in the New Year—though as a matter of fact I know of one vacancy going in Kamballa right now. In the Hot Chooks and Take-Away Tucker place,' she added with a wicked leer.

Eden, who had sat forward eagerly, subsided. That would be the last straw! Though, she reflected, there came a time when one had to clutch at even a last straw, and this just could be that time.

'Anyhow, I have a much better idea,' Amy said consolingly. 'It's been simmering in my mind ever since you landed on the doorstep. I thought even then that you just could be the answer to a maiden's prayer, only it didn't seem fair to stop you getting a job if you could. Well, you've had a good try now, haven't you? So look, Eden— I'm in a bit of a predicament. How would the idea of going over to the coast appeal to you?'

Eden's heart leapt hopefully. She'd love to go to the coast! All she'd seen of golden beaches and blue seas since she came to Australia had been from a plane. 'It appeals a lot. But what's your predicament?'

'I'll explain,' said Amy. 'The drawback is that it would only solve your problems for a month, then you'd be back where you started. And it's all sheer selfishness on my part, I warn you.'

23

'It's something to do with Burrangarra—this place where you're going,' guessed Eden when she paused. She was beginning to feel better already, and she kicked off her sandals and fanned her hair over the back of the sofa.

'That's right.' Amy got up to pour another drink for herself and do the same for Eden. 'At least, it's where I should be going. I'll tell you the whole story.' She flopped down on the floor again at Eden's feet and continued. 'You see, I contracted to look after my cousin Christie's bungalow—and her cat—for a month. Christie is one of my favourite people and I'd do anything for her, but this time I did have a funny sort of feeling I should live to regret my promise, and I have. Oh, I adore Christie—she's a dream and a darling, and beautiful as well. No one could be sweeter or more generous and full of kindness than Christie. And the darling admires me because I could always pass exams and she never could. She actually tried to be a nurse and it was going to be a tremendous battle, because nursing's just not all thermometers and bedpans, is it? Then she met this darling old business man from Brisbane who'd had his appendix out or something, and she married him. Not just out of kindness, or to get out of nursing. She loved him—she really did. And then he went and died on her after about three years, and she was terribly unhappy. Finally, she had to shift everything down to this holiday house at Burrangarra, really to get away from Brisbane—she had so many offers of marriage after poor William died. Everyone loves Christie, and except for William's dying, good luck's followed her all her life like a faithful hound. Oh—and she never had any children, but I suppose at his age, William wasn't all that keen on saddling her with a family.'

Eden listened, interested enough and vaguely amused, but anxious to know how she came into the picture.

'Anyhow,' resumed Amy, 'that's likely to be remedied

24

because now, at the ripe old age of twenty-five, she's met an absolute dreamboat of a man who's just perfect for her. A freelance journalist or something who's led a madly exciting life and now wants to settle down and write about it all—*and* the most gorgeous male you've ever set eyes on. Well, almost, anyhow. So of course she's madly happy.'

'She's married him?' asked Eden.

'Not yet. Not quite. And this is where we come in. She's off to Bangkok with him and his sister—today, come to think of it—for a month. Lorraine's engaged to a man there and he's being shifted back to Sydney, so they'll all come back to Australia together. I promised to go down to Burrangarra on Friday to mind the house and to release Khu Khan from three nights' incarceration in a pets' guest house. Poor little pusscat, he hates every minute of it, and Christie just adores him. It would break both their hearts if he had to stay there for a month instead of being in his own home.'

'And now,' Eden guessed, 'you want me to go instead?'

'Yes. But just to hold the fort for a few days, Eden, and then we can be there together and keep each other company. I adore summer on the coast, but I've been asked to a weekend party and I'm just dying to go.' She put a hand on her heart and made a comic face. 'His name's Malc Hewett, and I never thought he even knew I existed. But I've been invited for Saturday night and I'm to stay till Monday.'

Eden's mouth fell slightly open and Amy laughed.

'It's nothing immoral. He's a sheep farmer and a widower, and his place is sixty kilometres out of town. That's a long way for a young—attractive—single girl who's the teacher of your eight-year-old daughter to drive home on her own. But when the ball's over, I suppose I'll turn into a common old pumpkin again, and on Tuesday I'll be finding my way to Burrangarra. That is, if you'll stand in for me. If not—well, it's entirely up to you. I don't suppose Malc Hewett is really interested in me, not in the way I'd like, anyhow. It probably won't make any real difference to the course of my life if I can't go.'

'Oh, Amy, of course you must go! Of course I'll do it,' exclaimed Eden emphatically. 'It won't be any hardship, will it?' she added with a laugh.

'Thank you, Eden, you're a real friend,' Amy said. 'When I come I promise we'll have a marvellous time surfing and sunbaking and getting to know lots of people. After all, Malc Hewett and Berry Addison aren't the only males in existence, are they?'

Eden agreed that they weren't, but all the same she didn't think she'd be falling for the first male she met. You had to know a man really well before you fell even the slightest bit in love with him, she had decided.

A couple of days later, she and her luggage were loaded into a car that belonged to Ian Caster, a teacher at Amy's school. He and his wife Alice were heading for Murwillumbah to spend the summer vacation with Alice's parents, and as well as Eden a young man called Bill Hendry, who she discovered later was a sports master, was going along. Amy had arranged for Ian to call in at the pets' guest house before he dropped Eden off at Christie's bungalow, and Eden had dutifully rung her grandfather to tell him what she was doing. But it was not till almost the last moment that she learned something she found strangely disconcerting, and that was the name of Christie Vaughan's dreamboat.

It was Sinclair Watermount.

CHAPTER TWO

It really didn't matter, Eden reminded herself as Ian drove off and she turned to wave to Amy.

'I hope you won't be too lonely till I come,' Amy had said apologetically as they went downstairs to the car that was waiting at the kerb. 'It's a bit isolated at Birrie Point —just Christie's place and Sin Watermount's.'

'Sin Watermount's?' Eden had repeated hollowly, thinking she must be hearing things.

'Sin—short for Sinclair,' Amy explained, misinterpreting her reaction. 'He's Christie's boy-friend, but of course he's gone to Bangkok too, so you'll be all on your own for a few days.'

It was as though a shadow had passed across the sky, and ridiculously, Eden's mind leaped a month ahead, to the day when they would all come back—Christie, Lorraine, and *Sin*, who had seen her so belittled at Overlooking and probably thoroughly approved of the process. She just didn't want to be there.

Well, why worry about it now? she thought in the car. She'd surely be able to work it some way so that she could come back to Kamballa ahead of Amy. She'd get a lift from someone ...

It was a beautifully sunny day and a lovely drive, and the three others were agreeable and cheerful company, though Eden could have done with a little less admiring attention from Bill Hendry with whom she shared the back seat. He had friends in Murwillumbah, it appeared, and he too was going to spend his vacation there.

'How come I've never seen you around the place in

27

Kamballa, Eden?' he wanted to know. 'Or have you just come out from England?'

'I've been in Australia three and a half months,' Eden admitted. 'But I've been living out of town with my grandfather until just lately.'

'Then that explains it. I hope you're going to stay in town. Do you have a job of some sort lined up?'

'Not yet,' said Eden rather uncommunicatively. She wasn't in the mood for indulging in preliminaries to a possible future romance, if that was what Bill had in mind, and by the way he was looking at her she thought it was. She turned away from him and stared out at the countryside. Bill was certainly a very presentable-looking young man, tallish, well-built and as dark-haired as Berry Addison —to all appearances a very nice guy. But appearances, reflected Eden, weren't everything, and anyhow she was in no hurry, and there must be loads of nice guys around Australia, though just now she was feeling a trifle wary of them.

She kept on her own side of the seat and didn't have much to say as Ian drove on over the Great Divide, along a road that wound through ferny shady rain-forest, then through the steep green slopes where tropical fruits grew, and down and down to the narrow coastal plain with its dairy farms and timber mills. Then at last they were driving by the sparkling sapphire waters of the Pacific Ocean, already glimpsed from up in the ranges.

It was past noon when they reached Burrangarra, a small holiday and fishing town that stretched along the coast where the sea came in to a long beach of silver sand. Ian pulled up at the address Amy had given him, and Bill left the car with Eden while she collected Khu Khan—a Siamese cat with beautiful blue eyes and a narrow aristocratic face. He was presented to her in a pretty wicker basket lined with a quilted cushion, and he behaved like a

28

thorough gentleman. There was something eerily human in the loud miaow with which he greeted Eden, his rescuer.

'He knows you're taking him home,' said Alice when they were back in the car. 'Siamese cats are super-intelligent. I'll bet he's spoiled, though.'

Birrie Point was past the northern end of the beach, and before they got there they drove by the smooth waters of a long lagoon that snaked back of the shore, then past a cluster of holiday homes that Alice said belonged to people from inland. A side road cut in towards the steep and rocky headland that was Birrie Point, and there, almost hidden among the eucalypts and tea trees and banksias, they located Christie's bungalow.

Eden glanced anxiously around as Ian pulled up on a shady drive of fine yellowish gravel. There was one other bungalow on the point, not very far away, and she knew it must belong to Sinclair Watermount. The windows were shut and she turned away, feeling reassured.

'It's a beaut place for a holiday,' was Alice's verdict. 'Looks a nice bungalow too. Let's have a squizz! May we?'

'Of course,' agreed Eden, and all of them left the car to walk through the garden towards the house. Bill carried Eden's luggage and she carried Khu Khan in his basket. Ian put his arm around Alice and remarked, 'It could be pretty lonely here for a kid like you, Eden.'

'She'll have some sort of company—there's a bungalow next door,' said Alice practically. 'Any idea who lives there?'

Eden shrugged as if she hadn't; for some reason she didn't want to go into explanations—or to talk about Sin Watermount. Khu Khan was miaowing plaintively, so she let him out of his basket and he bounded off into the garden.

Christie's house was white-painted timber, with wide eaves that shaded garden furniture and pot plants. The front door was pea-green, and was studded a little ostentatiously with decorative copper rosettes. Eden found the key where Amy had said it would be—in a big green potplant not far from the door—and unlocked the door. The others trooped in with her to look around, and Bill wondered aloud, 'Why am I going to Murwillumbah? This place has plenty going for it. Couldn't you do with a bit of company, Eden? Just don't be surprised if I nip down the coast and pay you a visit one day, will you? You'll stay on with Amy when she comes, of course.'

'For a while, anyhow,' Eden agreed cautiously. 'I don't really have any definite plans.'

'How about next year? You'll be back in Kamballa——'

'Oh, come on, blokey,' said Alice good-humouredly from the front door. 'You don't have to line up all your dates yet—Eden's not going to melt away like a block of ice— she'll keep.'

A couple of minutes later Eden had waved goodbye to them, gone inside, and was on her own. She had a feeling that Bill had had ideas about kissing her goodbye, but she had seen that it didn't happen. She just wasn't going to start anything.

Khu Khan had streaked into the house ahead of her, and Eden discovered him in the living room where he had installed himself self-indulgently on the coral pink couch. It was a pretty room, all pink and pale champagne, with a touch of soft water-green in the cushions and floor rugs. Wide windows looked down through the bush towards the sea, and open shelves displayed a few books, a pile of magazines, and a multitude of small ornaments including numerous glass and ceramic animals. There were a few framed prints on the walls and she recognised Renoir's little girl with a watering can, and Picasso's pretty 'Child with a pigeon'.

Continuing with her general appraisal, Eden suddenly

stopped dead in the middle of the room. Regarding her from the top of a writing desk by a side window was a large framed photograph of Sinclair Watermount. His gaze unnerved her more than slightly, though it was not the unflattering regard she had encountered at Overlooking. She looked back at him appraisingly. A gorgeous male, Amy had said. An absolute dreamboat. And it was Sinclair Watermount! In the bottom right-hand corner something was scrawled blackly, and moving closer, she read the single word, 'Sin'. Not much of a message for the woman you loved, she thought dryly, and almost without conscious thought she turned the portrait face down.

There were two other photographs displayed in the room. One was of an elderly man whom she took to be Christie's father till she read the neat unflamboyant inscription—'For my darling Christie, from William'. Eden felt a little shock of surprise. He looked so old! The other picture was a blown-up colour print of Christie herself—who else could it be?—standing with Sin Watermount on the beach against a background of white scalloped waves.

Christie was certainly very, very attractive. She wore a pale blue denim shirt and matching jeans, her eyes were dreamy and her blonde hair flowed out in the wind. Eden thought there was a sort of listening look on her face, curiously childlike. Sin, beside her, was smiling amusedly at whoever took the photograph. Well, that photograph could stay where it was; it was small enough not to haunt her. Besides, she couldn't go round turning everything in Christie's house upside down just to humour her own hang-ups.

Eden headed for the small kitchen, thinking of lunch, and Khu Khan, possibly hungry too, followed her, rubbing his sleek coat affectionately against her legs and pulling up suggestively in front of the refrigerator.

'What am I going to give you to eat?' she asked him, looking around her. The kitchen was separated from the dining section of the living room by a long white-topped counter ornamented by a huge pink copper jug that held hydrangeas which plainly needed water. On the counter as well as a sheet of paper with a message for Amy on it.

'Dearest Amy,' Eden read, 'Welcome to my little house. Please make yourself at home. Have a lovely time and don't worry about housework, the cleaning lady is taking a holiday but will do a grand clean-up as soon as I get back. There's still food in the fridge, and the freezer is crammed, so eat up! Some money in the Chinese vase in the sitting room, so *use* it. Chuck steak for Khu, but give him fish now and again, he loves it. Feed the darling at night—he drinks water not milk—and give him Kitty Bikkies in the mornings or when he's really persuasive. It will keep him away from the birds! I let him sleep on my bed, so he'll probably expect the same privilege from you —you can sort that out for yourself. Please take my car for a run now and again so the battery won't go flat—keys in Chinese vase. Some friends have promised to look you up—the Websters—so you won't be lonely. You might even fall in love with Don—he's nice! Love, Christie.'

Fairly comprehensive, thought Eden. But Amy wasn't going to fall in love with Don—and nor was she, come to that. She found Khu Khan's biscuits and put some in a flowery dish and filled a matching bowl with water. She had brought tomato sandwiches from Amy's flat for herself, and she found evaporated milk and instant coffee and was soon enjoying her lunch by the big windows, and looking out through the garden. She couldn't see the beach from here—it was way below the edge of the headland—but the sea had lost its clear jewel blue colour and was now tinged with indigo and beginning to look pretty rough. Possibly a storm was brewing, and if she wanted to explore she had better get a move on.

She finished her lunch, changed into shorts and a pink top, slipped her bare feet into rubber thong sandals and went out, carefully locking the door behind her and hiding the key away in the green pot. Khu Khan had come outside too, but he didn't follow her, preferring to stay and re-discover his favourite haunts in the garden. Christie's garden was mostly natural bush, and the ground was thick with leaves and strips of bark from the gum trees. Tiny bluish dragonflies drifted about in the air like flimsy flickering flames as Eden went through the trees, which were now moving in the wind. She followed a path and reached the beginning of a track that led steeply down to the beach —a small crescent of silver, very secret and private-looking. She made her way down carefully and finally jumped on to soft white sand. The beach was completely deserted, and the only sounds were the screaming of the seagulls and the booming of the waves that came racing in to shore.

An hour or so later she was hurrying back to clamber into the shelter of the tea trees. There were low purple clouds all across the sky and a few big drops of rain had fallen, and she pushed her way upwards through prickly bush, finally to emerge gasping at the top of Birrie Point, There the need for haste vanished. She discovered she was right on the edge of Christie's dreamboat's garden. If it did rain bucketsful she wouldn't have far to go for shelter—and it was likely to rain bucketsful, she realised, for Amy had warned her that tropical thunderstorms were part of the summer at Burrangarra.

Meanwhile, she looked curiously in the direction of Sin Watermount's bungalow. 'I'll just have a squizz,' she thought, copying the phrase Alice had used that morning, and she trotted gaily through the garden, her thongs flapping against her heels.

It was an attractive bungalow in dark oiled timber that blended in with the bush. Soon Eden was walking warily across a stone-paved patio and into the shelter of a slightly sloping roof made of what looked like reinforced glass. Hydrangeas and geraniums tumbled from big pots, and a low stone lamp that looked like something from a Japanese garden guarded a small pool where there were goldfish and waterlilies. Somehow, Eden couldn't quite convince herself that it all belonged to that tough and rugged-looking individual, Sin Watermount. She must be making a mistake! There were so many intriguing little touches—like the windbells made of crinkly pink pearl shells by one of the doors, and a carved stone head of the Buddha. There were tall banana palms, and yellow ginger blossoms with stamens like red-hot needles scented the air seductively.

Some bright parrots flew overhead suddenly as if startled, and their quick excited screeching was like the high-pitched clinking of shells being tumbled on the shore. Eden had forgotten the approaching thunderstorm and had cupped her hands around her face to peer inquisitively in at one of the windows when thunder began in a deep growl that rattled the glass. Almost simultaneously something heavy fell on her shoulder—a hand, she soon discovered! —and a voice demanded coldly, 'What in the name of seven devils do you think you're doing?'

Her face scarlet, her heart pounding at the unexpectedness of it, she turned and found herself confronting—oh, horror—Sin Watermount. The disgust in his eyes was plain to see, and her heart sank abysmally as she realised she must be confirming the impression he had already formed of her at Overlooking. Too late she wished she had kept away from his windows and saved herself the humiliation of being caught out prying. But what on earth was he doing here? Undoubtedly he must be wondering the same thing about her. Ridiculously, she heard herself stammer out, 'Aren't you—aren't you in Bangkok?'

His wide mouth twisted up at one corner. 'What do you think? And isn't it more to the point for me to be asking the questions? This happens to be my house and I'd very much like to know what you're doing hanging about and pressing your busy little nose against my window panes.'

She quaked inwardly at his tone—it seemed lately that she just couldn't win. But she said pertly, almost echoing his own words, 'Well, what would you think? I'm—I'm just looking, that's all.' Her eyes flicked over him uneasily, and she saw that he wore a close-fitting pink shirt open almost to the waist, and against the darkish hairs on his chest a fine gold chain glittered menacingly. Actually it was his eyes that were glittering menacingly, she corrected that thought as she reluctantly raised her own.

'You're certainly doing that. But just what enticed you to this part of the world?' he persisted.

For this part read my part, she thought, and said with a touch of defiance, 'I'm looking after the house next door, as it happens.'

He stared at her unbelievingly. 'Oh, come on now! That can't be possible. I understood that the amiable Amy was to be chatelaine.' His voice had roughened and he looked exasperated enough to shake her. 'Where *is* Amy?—if you know who I'm talking about.'

'Oh, be quiet!' she exclaimed furiously. 'Of course I know who you're talking about. Amy's a friend of mine. She can't get away for a few days and I'm helping her out. Though I'd have thought twice about it if I'd known you'd be around.'

'I can well believe that,' he said grimly. 'You didn't cut a pretty picture on the one occasion we met before, did you?—playing ducks and drakes while your grandfather was away. I'd say Amy had made a very questionable choice when she asked you to stand in for her.' His glance sharpened as he gestured with his head towards Christie's house. 'Are you alone up there?'

Her cheeks were fiery. He was suggesting that Berry Addison was there, and that was the limit! 'Yes, I'm alone. And I wish I were even more so. I was assured you'd gone to Bangkok.'

'Unfortunately for both of us, I have not gone to Bangkok. I was, however, planning to go to Canberra in a few days' time. In the meantime, be sure I shan't force my company on you, though I warn you I might call in to check up now and again.' They stared at each other and Eden was quivering with anger and dislike. 'It's going to rain like the devil any minute now, so why don't you scoot off back next door?'

'That's just what I'm going to do. And I wish you'd scoot off to Canberra.' She was slightly appalled at the way her tongue was running away with her, but he was being so unpleasant—she couldn't just sit back and take it. 'Why didn't you go to Thailand anyhow?' she asked rather weakly.

'Because I happen to have some rather pressing work on hand. Does that satisfy you?'

'What sort of work?' she asked suspiciously.

'I'm writing a book. Nothing that would interest you. And I discover I need to do some research.'

Eden considered that for a second. Imagine passing up a month in Bangkok with your girl-friend just because of work! Especially when it was all planned. He had probably been to Bangkok already, of course—hadn't Amy said he'd had a madly exciting life? She was about to ask a further question when the rain that had been threatening began to fall in a torrent, pelting on the glass roof so deafeningly that it would be useless to try to talk. The sea, the bush, were blotted out, and Khu Khan came streaking on to the

36

patio as though chased by a bunyip. Same under shelter, he proceeded to lick the rain meticulously from his beautiful and priceless fur with an efficient pink tongue.

Eden glanced sideways at Sin Watermount and made a little face. She couldn't scoot off home in this! Though come to think of it, she wouldn't put it past him to insist. He didn't, however, but nor did he invite her inside, and they stood without speaking, listening to the rain and thinking their own thoughts. The noise had lessened slightly when he moved closer to her and asked sharply, 'What's your name?'

'Eden Dare.'

'Hm. Your mother is a Pomeroy, I take it, and your father an Englishman. And you've come out here to visit your wealthy grandfather. Is that right?'

'If you say so,' she said with a shrug. She wasn't going to waste time telling him the story of her life when he could dream it up for himself.

'And now you've blotted your copybook and the good times are over.'

'And it serves me right, doesn't it?' put in Eden sweetly.

'I would say so,' he agreed without a second's pause, so if she had hoped to disconcert him she had failed.

'But thanks to Amy you've fallen on your feet,' he resumed after a second. 'Well, I advise you to take your responsibilities here seriously, Eden Dare, and not to imagine that your liability begins and ends with seeing that Christie's animal is housed and fed.'

She stared at him with hostility, because there was Khu Khan, so blue-eyed and aristocratic and perfect, grooming himself fastidiously, and this man had called him an animal! 'You mean Khu Khan, I presume,' she said coldly.

He shrugged that off with an ironic look and pursued, 'I daresay it won't even occur to you to flick around with a duster now and again, but bear this in mind—whatever's in that house is in your custody and you'll be held responsible for it.'

She flushed at his emphasis. For heaven's sake—did he imagine she was going to take the pictures off the walls, the knick-knacks off the shelves, or sneak around the place seeing what she could pocket? She was an ordinary decent honest girl, and one day she would tell him the truth about that incident at Overlooking. And he wouldn't believe her, of course . . .

'Have you met Christie?' The question shot into her thoughts.

She wished she could confound him and say that she had met Christie and that Christie liked her and trusted her and believed in her integrity. But she hadn't ever met Christie, so——

Before she could answer at all he said irritably, 'Well, make up your mind. It's a simple question that requires yes or no for an answer. I can't believe that you're so used to tampering with the truth that even a straight-out question of that kind presents tempting possibilities in deception.'

Eden said coldly, 'No, I haven't met Christie, but I know Amy well. Actually, I was wondering what the point of your interrogation was. After all, it's an arrangement that needn't concern you at all.'

He didn't contradict her, though she supposed in all fairness he could have pointed out that whatever concerned Christie concerned him. The next moment, the rain had stopped as suddenly as if a tap had been turned off, and Eden took the opportunity to go.

'Thanks for allowing me to shelter outside your precious house,' she said rather pointedly. 'Goodbye for now.' She stooped to gather up Khu Khan and ran quickly through the garden and across the bush which, extraordinarily, had actually begun to steam as the sun came bursting through the heavens and struck the ground blindingly.

'Forget him,' she told herself firmly as she rooted out the key and let herself into the house. Of course it rankled to have someone think you were a very low form of life, but there was nothing to be done except carry on as though he didn't exist. And in this particular case, it appeared she didn't merely have to hope that if she didn't look he would go away. Happily, he was really going—to Canberra, to do his research, she supposed, for a book that wouldn't interest her. And he was right, it wouldn't—not if *he* was writing it.

In the meantime, if he came snooping round, then she hoped she would not be at home. She determined, in fact, to spend all the time she could on the beach. And in a few days Amy would be here, though by that time, God willing, Sin Watermount would have gone ...

She watched his movements the next day, feeling rather like a spy. As he was a writer she supposed he would work at home, which was a pity. The first thing that she discovered was that he went for an early morning swim.

Drinking a cup of coffee at six in the morning over by the big windows, she could see someone swimming far out beyond the breakers. She was certain it must be Sin Watermount, and having noticed some field-glasses on the shelf, she used them to take a look and recognised him clearly as he swam parallel with the shore, using a long, powerful, purposeful-looking stroke. Eden itched to be down there too. The sky was a miracle of blue, completely cloudless, and she could feel a burningly hot day coming up. This would be the ideal time to swim. She had never surfed in her life and yesterday she had thought the waves looked enticing. But it would be a lot more fun—and a lot safer too—if she had someone to keep her company. Failing that, she must make the best of it on her own until Amy came.

39

She heated some rolls she had found packaged in the freezer and had a continental-type breakfast, keeping an eye on the sea while she did so. She looked after Khu Khan, rinsed the dishes, then got into her bathing suit—a navy blue one-piece that made her already slender figure look even more slender. Thus clad, she did a little dusting. 'Flicked around with a duster,' she thought, annoyed at the memory of what Sin Watermount had said. One tall narrow cupboard in the kitchen was neatly stacked with cleaning apparatus, and Eden was determined to have the whole place looking spotless when Amy came. She dusted the shelves in the living room with the greatest of care, admiring the multiplicity of ornaments as she did so. The portrait of Sin Watermount she touched with the duster, then left it lying on its face. She had made her bed and tidied her bedroom, and put her things away carefully so no one would know she was even occupying it. Her mother had taught her tidiness. Their house had been very small, and it was a habit that had stood her in good stead at Overlooking, though her grandfather had never given even grudging praise when she kept his house spick and span. He took it for granted, of course. It was part of woman's purpose in life to serve important males such as himself.

When she returned to the living room later, there was no sign of anyone in the sea. It was after seven-thirty, and she hoped that Sin Watermount was in his own bungalow having his breakfast. With this hope held to her heart, she put on a long shirt over her swimsuit, picked up her towel and went down to the beach, taking care not even to turn her head in the direction of the other bungalow.

The beach looked a dream, clean and washed and virgin, despite the blackish rocks towards the far end. And of course there were footprints there, aggressive, widely spaced, and as firm as that black signature that said, uncompromisingly, *Sin*. She could find the exact place where he had tossed his towel down before he went into the water, and deliberately she chose a spot some distance away. The water still had an early morning sparkle on it, though the sun was hot on her bare shoulders as she waded into the sea, feeling the lap and slap of the waves against her legs. Further out, she plunged beneath a wave and found the water suddenly deep. The sun was bright in her eyes as she struck out, aiming to get beyond the breakers where she could swim—as he had done. But it wasn't easy. The waves were big and their will was stronger than hers, and eventually she gave up and contented herself staying close to the shore.

It was not till she was coming out, stepping high through the water as she felt the backward drag of the waves, that the thought struck Eden that Sin might see her from his window just as she had seen him. That she didn't like, because she was no surfer. 'Forget him,' she told herself not for the first time, and picking up her towel she proceeded to rub her head vigorously before she wiped her limbs down.

Now what? Sunbathing? And where, she wondered, looking about her wryly, were all those sun-bronzed heroes that Amy had at least intimated would be sporting about on the beach? There was no one there at all. She had the whole beach to herself.

She lay on her face in the hand and dozed a little, lulled by the wish-wash and the crunch of the waves. She had no idea what time it was when she finally sat up, staggered to her feet, and feeling distinctly baked, headed back towards the house. She had some shopping to do. She wasn't going to eat up all Christie's frozen foods, and she wanted fresh fruit and bread and milk—and besides, it was lonely in the house with only Khu Khan for company. He, she thought —meaning Sin—would be engrossed in his work in the other bungalow. It was funny to think of him sitting down at a typewriter and tapping away when he was such a big husky hunk of masculinity. She would never in a million years have guessed him to be a writer.

She gasped when she found him standing, arms folded, in the shadows of the bush after she had climbed up from the beach.

'Good morning,' he said abruptly, and almost impersonally his heavy-browed, greenish eyes took in her long naked legs, her straggling salty hair, her flushed face where the freckles would be showing up as they always did when she had been in the sun. 'Just a word of advice——'

'I don't need any more,' she interrupted swiftly, and brushing past him, stooped to shake a twig out of her thongs. His hand whipped out to grip her as she straightened.

'I'm not asking you about that. You'll listen whether you like it or not. And I advise you not to go swimming at the beach down there.'

'Because of sharks?' she asked scornfully. 'From what I've read, I'm more likely to be injured in a car accident than to be molested by a shark. I'll take my luck with everyone else where sharks are concerned.' Actually she hadn't given a thought to sharks, and she felt a shiver of fear run over her limbs as she spoke.

His eyebrows lifted. He was wearing faded blue denim pants and a shirt with the sleeves pushed up. His and hers, she thought ironically, thinking of the photograph of Christie.

'Because of the cruelty of the sea,' he said, ignoring her remarks. 'You don't know the tides or the currents here— any of the treacherous moods of this particular bay. You just could find yourself carried out to sea and unable to get back. I don't spend all my time at the window, and even if I did, I mightn't be able to get to your rescue in time. In future, do your swimming in the lagoon or off the

42

beach in Burrangarra where there are plenty of people. You'll make some friends that way too—but choose them with care, and don't go bringing every Tom, Dick and Harry home to a house that doesn't belong to you.'

What a role he cast her in! She was certainly the naughtiest girl in the school. She said cynically, 'You swim off the beach down here, Mr Watermount, so what's the matter? Am I invading your privacy? I'm not completely stupid. If the sea's too rough I shan't go in. I can look after myself. And don't,' she concluded, 'try telling me how to choose my friends. I can——'

He had closed his eyes and now he opened them again. 'I've already seen a sample of the kind of man you fall for— a type your grandfather has to hunt off. Christie Vaughan happens to be a friend of mine, and you're occupying her house——'

'Oh, I know all that.' She pushed past him and closed her ears, and as she continued on her way she tried to shake off the sound of his voice and the look in his eyes.

Inside, she showered and changed into cotton shirt and jeans and made herself a cool drink, then contemplated the prospect of the long walk into town to do her shopping. In the growing heat it was hardly enticing, and she remembered Christie's note telling Amy to use her car. She had her driver's licence as a matter of fact. She had got it in England, but her grandfather had never allowed her to drive since she had come to Australia. But she would be crazy to walk when a car was available, and she could take it slowly till she got the feel of it. She wasn't very experienced, but she couldn't possibly come to any harm just driving that short distance on a quiet road, into a quiet coastal town.

She tipped up the Chinese vase and found the key, and a whole bundle of notes as well. Over two hundred dollars, she discovered, and stuffed them away out of sight again.

She had a little money, and she would have few expenses. That money could stay there until Amy came, and then it would be out of her hands whether they used it or not.

The car was in a garage at the side of the house. It was sleek and shining, and a shimmering golden beige. It looked practically new and Eden looked at it with faint awe. Dared she? It had been backed into the garage, so it would simply be a matter of driving out. Why not, then? She climbed in and discovered it was an automatic, so what could be easier? In a moment she had started it up and putting her foot gently on the accelerator, she was thrilled to feel the car glide gently forward. She was halfway down the drive when Sin Watermount suddenly materialised to stand, hands on hips, straight ahead of her. Eden drove steadily on and he didn't budge, and fuming inwardly she was forced to pull up. She leaned out of the window and said firmly but reasonably, 'Please get out of my way. I have my licence if you're wondering, and Christie specifically asked to have the car used.'

'By Amy,' he said with a disagreeable smile. 'Not by unknown and irresponsible little girls ... What's your problem? Do you need to go out or are you just looking for some way to amuse yourself?'

'What do you think? I have to eat, don't I? I need to do some shopping,' she told him angrily. To tell the truth, her self-confidence was a little shaken too. It *was* taking on quite a responsibility to drive someone else's car. All the same, he had no right to tell her what she might or might not do. 'Will you please move?' she demanded. 'You surely don't expect me to trudge into town in this heat.'

'It wouldn't do you all that much harm,' he said annoyingly. He moved quickly and opened the car door. 'Move over,' he commanded. 'I'll do the driving.'

Eden hung on to the wheel determinedly. But what was

the use of protesting? He won, of course, through sheer force.

She said absolutely nothing as they drove through the bush to the road that ran down from the headland, past the lagoon, and so to Burrangarra. There he pulled up in the main shopping street which to her surprise was quite busy.

'Right.' He looked at his watch. 'I'll give you forty minutes to get your shopping done and be back here. Get moving. I don't like to have my working hours interrupted.'

She very nearly said 'I'm sorry', and then she remembered that she hadn't interrupted his working hours. She said with a bright smile, 'If you kept your head down, Mr Watermount, you wouldn't have been interrupted. You shouldn't have been so interested in—in spying on me. I assure you your interest isn't returned.'

'Oh, cut along,' he said impatiently.

Eden departed. And it wasn't really because she had made up her mind to keep him waiting that it was close on an hour before she got back. It was mainly because she didn't yet know her way around. She was almost surprised when she got back to find him still there—smoking and staring ahead of him with a rather worried frown on his face.

When he took her back he handed her the keys once the car was in the garage, though she had more or less expected that he would keep them.

'Get all you want?' he asked absently before he turned away towards his own bungalow.

'Yes,' she said, and added stiffly, 'Thank you for the lift.'

A gleam of surprise showed briefly in his eyes, but he nodded curtly. 'Think nothing of it. I'll be seeing you.'

'Not if I can help it,' thought Eden. But she didn't say it aloud.

CHAPTER THREE

THAT evening at about five o'clock, Eden heard Sin's car and saw that he was going out—probably for dinner somewhere, she thought. She didn't imagine he was heading for Canberra. No such luck!

At all events, she took the opportunity to go down to the beach and enjoy the cool sea breeze there, because the day had been a scorcher. She was back just as it was beginning to grow dark, and Khu Khan appeared from the shadows and brushed against her bare legs as she found the key and let herself in. She fed the cat and had a light meal herself, then switched on the radio and listened to some music. Christie had a colour television set, but she wasn't in the mood for TV. Christie, in fact, appeared to have just about everything—and now she had her dreamboat as well. Only for some reason he hadn't been able to go to Bangkok with her. And that was a great shame—as far as Eden Dare was concerned.

She listened to the music and looked through the window at the string of lights of another small town away beyond the rocky point on the far side of the little beach. —Birrie Beach, she had discovered from one of the shopkeepers that morning. She had learned too that Birrie was an aboriginal word meaning danger.

'Danger from what?' she had asked, and had been told, 'Rips—big tides. There've been several drownings there.'

So she had better take some notice of what Sin Watermount said after all, though it did rather go against the grain.

He hadn't gone to Canberra. Next morning she saw him

swimming in his sea out beyond the breakers. Did he like taking risks, or could she conclude that the sea was in a benign mood when she saw him out there? Well, she would watch it. She didn't particularly fancy being carried out to sea and drowned, but it was a long way to walk to the lagoon and further still to Burrangarra, so she would swim at Birrie Beach but stay close in to the shore.

The water looked smooth and sparkling and harmless when she went down later in the morning. The cicadas were singing in the heat and the day was absolutely heavenly— if you were as lucky as Eden Dare and had nothing to do but swim or lie about in the sun. The problem of how she was to support herself now she no longer had a home with her grandfather had receded—she wasn't going to worry about it until this idyll was over.

She tossed down her towel and her book and her sunglasses and tripped down to the water. White gulls pattered silently on the smooth wet sand and she waded into the waves, enjoying their cool touch. It wasn't a big surf today, yet she soon discovered that there was an insidious and persistent strength in the undertow that had to be resisted. And despite her awareness of it, she was drifting slowly but surely towards some blackish rocks that lurked in the water. Just in case Sin Watermount should be watching her —and he was, she knew later—she allowed herself to drift deliberately, and clambered up on to the rocks as if that had been her object. She stood there in the sun for several minutes before plunging back into the water and making for the shore.

For the remainder of the morning she lay on the sand soaking up the sun till finally sheer hunger drove her home.

She had made a salad and some coffee, and still in her swimsuit was about to carry it to some shady spot outside, when the doorbell rang. She dumped the tray on a coffee table and went to the door to find Sin Watermount there. He raised his eyebrows at the swimsuit and she coloured furiously and demanded, 'What do you want? I thought you'd be working. I suppose you've come to check up on me—you're always booted and spurred, aren't you? Well, come along in—everything's still here, all the pictures—the knick-knacks—the lot—and nothing up my sleeve.'

She stopped and stood back, glaring at him, and though she didn't expect it, he calmly walked past her and through to the living room, where he deposited a couple of letters on the telephone table.

'Christie's mail. You should have checked the letter box.' He glanced at her lunch tray. 'Drink your coffee before it gets cold.'

'Why? Do you intend to stay long?'

'No longer than necessary.'

'Then carry on with your inspection and get it over.' She had half a mind to dash to the bedroom for a shirt, but then she thought, 'Blow him—I don't care what he thinks'. And instead she curled herself up in one of the arm-chairs within reach of her lunch tray. She sipped her coffee, ate some of her salad, and watched him without speaking, wishing he didn't have the effect of making her so horribly aggressive. She really would have to try harder to control her tongue!

He had an eagle eye and she was positive he knew every single thing that was on Christie's shelves. When he peered inside the Chinese vase she said acidly, 'Count it if you want to—it's all there.'

'A fat wad of notes,' he commented, virtually ignoring her, 'even Christie wouldn't know how much. I've told her not to do that.'

He strolled over to the writing desk where his portrait lay face down, and through her lashes she watched for his reaction to that. He stood the frame upright with the in-dolent question, 'What have you got to hide?'

'Nothing,' she said promptly. 'I just see enough of you as it is.'

'It could be a reminder,' he suggested.

'A reminder about what?'

'That I'm around—if your principles start slipping,' he said dryly.

'Oh, I know you're around,' she snapped, her resolutions forgotten. 'I hear your sword clinking day and night.'

He smiled slightly and Eden swallowed her fury and con-centrated on her salad, and he went to stand with his back to the windows and to look at her through narrowed eyes.

'You found out something about the sea this morning, didn't you?' he asked conversationally.

She widened her grey eyes and stared at him unblink-ingly. 'Did I? What?'

'That it has a will of its own. That is can look harmless yet carry you somewhere you don't want to be before you know what's happening. It's as capricious as love and almost as dangerous, if you like to look at it that way. Per-haps you're willing now to concede that my warning wasn't just selfishness, or do you like playing with danger?'

Eden bit her lip. Why bring love into it? 'Maybe I do,' she said obstinately. 'Have you finished now? And have you any complaints? I know picking holes is your favourite occupation.'

He screwed up one eye and looked at her quizzically. 'Then I'll pick one now. Next time you go out, you might take care to lock the outside doors.'

'I do,' she retorted.

'The front door,' he agreed, 'the obvious one. But not the other.'

The back door? But she'd never so much as opened the

back door. If that hadn't been locked, then surely Christie was to blame. On the point of telling him so, she paused. He wouldn't believe her—she could picture the cynical look that would come into those assessing eyes of his. And anyhow, it wouldn't be fair to tell tales on Christie. She was his girl-friend, and it must be decidedly difficult to live up to the rigorous standards of Sin Watermount. One more bad mark against Eden Dare's name wasn't going to matter all that much.

'Or did you by any chance leave that door unlocked on purpose? Are you expecting a visitor?'

A man, he meant, of course. Berry Addison.

'I'm expecting no one,' she said tightly. 'Only Amy. And everyone forgets something now and again. Except you,' she added, and immediately wished she hadn't.

His eyebrows rose. 'It's irresponsible to take your kind of forgetting for granted. And for your information, for Christie's protection I shan't go to Canberra until this place is in more reliable hands. Such as Amy's.'

'Then that means,' said Eden, scooping up the last of her salad and looking at him with wide blank eyes in which he could read what he liked, 'that you'll be snooping around here till Tuesday. Well, it's not all that long.'

His tilted eyebrows suggested that to him it was an infinity, but he moved towards the door and from there told her casually, 'By the way, if you want the shops or some safe swimming and some pleasant company, my sister's bicycle is at my bungalow. You may borrow it.'

Surprised, she tilted her eyebrows back at him and smiled distantly. 'I don't want it, thank you, Mr Watermount. I can get by without any side benefits from you.'

'As you wish. But I hope you'll have the good sense to leave the car alone.'

She didn't answer, and he turned and went.

Back to his typewriter, she supposed, and wondered what

kind of a book he was writing. Something as dry as dust, she could be sure of that, and far too intellectual for her. Well, that could be so. Since she left school her time had been pretty well taken up with looking after her mother and the handicrafts shop. She hadn't had the leisure to read anything very heavy . . .

During the afternoon the Websters turned up, and Eden felt an almost foolish sense of pleasure. It *was* lonely here, and now there were these two people, somewhere about her own age—Don and his sister Bibi. Don was good-looking and very personable, Bibi—well, somehow a bit less personable but full of bounce and go and self-confidence. When she answered the door they both smiled at her, and it was the girl who spoke.

'Hello! I'm Bibi Webster and this is my brother Don— Christie probably told you about us. You're Amy Blythe, aren't you?'

Eden smiled back at them both. 'Hello! Please do come in. I'm not Amy, as a matter of fact, I'm a friend of hers, Eden Dare.' She ushered them into the living room, continuing on the way, 'Amy isn't here yet. She had a couple of important dates, so I'm sort of holding the fort till she's free. Do sit down.'

Don took a chair, but Bibi strolled over to the writing desk and took a look at Sin Watermount's portrait before she sat down. Eden thought it a bit odd, but felt thankful it hadn't been lying face down. She'd forgotten about it since Sin was here. . .

Bibi was a tall girl with straight shortish coppery hair, a load more freckles than Eden had, a full lower lip and brown shining eyes. Her wide-necked blouse and tawny brown skirt showed off a shapely bosom and a very narrow waist. 'Not much older than me,' Eden thought, 'but she's got a load more worldly knowledge.'

Don offered cigarettes, and when both refused, put them

away. Bibi perched on the arm of the sofa and swung one bare leg.

'You're a friend of Christie's, are you?' she asked Eden.

'Well, I've never met her, actually. Amy and I are friends.'

'Oh. When will Amy be here?'

'On Tuesday, I think.'

'Will you stay on?'

'Yes. It will be company for Amy.'

Don, who had removed his sunglasses, looked across at her. 'My parents wanted to invite Amy to spend Christmas Day with us. Of course the invitation will include you too, now. What do you think? You haven't made any other plans, have you?'

'No. I'd love to come—and I'm sure Amy would too. It's very kind of you. But are you sure about me? I mean, two people instead of one——'

'Oh, that will be all right. My mother would insist, I know. I suppose you have a car?'

'Amy has,' Eden nodded.

'Well, we're at Nepelle Heights. It's on a turn-off from the main road up the ranges. There's a sign—you can't miss it. But if you decide you need more details we're on the phone ... I suppose you've been finding it lonely on your own.'

'A little. It's nice to have you here. But I love the beach —this is my first visit to the coast.'

'You're English, of course,' Bibi commented as though the thought had only just struck her. 'Are you here for a holiday or for keeps?'

'I'm not quite sure. I came out to live with my aunt, but she died before I arrived, and—well, my grandfather and I just don't really hit it off.'

'Shame,' murmured Bibi abstractedly. Her eyes had been darting around the room as busy as dragonflies, whereas

52

Don didn't seem very interested in his surroundings at all.

'I'll make some tea, shall I?' Eden asked, rising to her feet.

'Great. I could do with a cup,' Bibi agreed, and as Eden turned away she suddenly exclaimed excitedly, 'Good lord! That can't be Sin Watermount! Didn't he go to Bangkok with his sister? And Christie,' she added.

'He apparently had too much work to do,' said Eden briefly. She had turned to look through the window too and to her dismay she saw that Sin was striding towards the bungalow—to see who her visitors were, no doubt.

'He'll be surprised when he sees us here,' remarked Bibi with a giggle. Her cheeks were slightly flushed. 'Don's only had that car about a week.' Her eyes suddenly explored Eden's face. 'Have you seen much of Sin?'

'Very little,' said Eden—though she could have said 'Too much'. 'I think he spends most of his time working.' The doorbell rang and she went to let him in.

He stood in the doorway—aggressive, sexy, swaggering, jaw jutting, that gold chain visible against a bronzed chest that was completely bare as he wore only beach shorts and sandals.

'Yes, Mr Watermount?' Eden kept her voice low and sweet. 'Do you want me to muster my visitors for an inspection?'

He didn't have to answer that because Bibi came bouncing to the door.

'*Sin!* You didn't go to Thailand! How marvellous to see you! I can't believe it! Are you coming in?' Just as though, thought Eden, taken aback, she owned the place.

Sin looked at Eden in mocking inquiry. 'May I? As you can see, I'm hardly dressed for visiting.'

She coloured with annoyance. 'It doesn't matter. Come in, of course. I was just going to make some tea.'

Don rose briefly when they went back inside. He sent

Sin a nod and a brief, 'How's it going?' before he sat down again.

'We came to look up Christie's cousin,' explained Bibi, still excited. 'Oh, it's great to see you! What happened about Bangkok?' Her eyes were bright with curiosity and with something else that Eden couldn't interpret.

'I just couldn't make it,' Sin said. 'It was a bit doubtful from the start, and I discovered I had a lot more work on my hands than I liked. More research to do, too—I'll be leaving for Canberra within the next few days.'

'Stay for Christmas,' pleaded Bibi. 'Spend the day with us. Amy will be coming and—er——'

'Eden,' supplied Sin, settling in a chair.

'Yes, Eden too ... you can stay till Christmas Day, surely, Sin.'

He shook his head regretfully. 'I doubt it. But——'

Eden didn't hear the rest. She moved off to the kitchen to make the tea, and though she could hear the murmur of their voices—mostly Bibi's and Sin's, she didn't think Don had much to say—she couldn't hear what they were talking about. Bibi certainly seemed to find Sin Watermount a likeable person, she reflected as she set out cups and saucers on a tray. She appeared to be on the friendliest possible terms with him, though Don was rather quiet and withdrawn. He—Don—wasn't really Amy's type, she decided, recalling that Christie had seemed eager to encourage a romance there.

She carried in the tray and poured the tea while the others continued to talk—about Burrangarra, and fishing, and fruit growing. She gathered that Bibi did the bookwork at her father's banana plantation and was far from enthusiastic about it.

'I feel just so cooped up there—I want to get out and see the world—travel,' she remarked as Eden handed her a cup and offered the biscuits. 'You're lucky, Sin—you

54

lead just the sort of life I envy. You've been everywhere.'

'By no means,' he said with a smile, and he sent Bibi a look that rather rocked Eden. She was sure that Christie wouldn't like to see Sin look at another girl that way. He rose to take his cup from Eden. 'Frankly, I'm happy to settle down in one place for a while ... How are things progressing at Nepelle Heights?' he asked, sitting down again and addressing Don.

Bibi, with a grimace, answered the question before her brother could speak. 'Oh, summer's the worst possible time to live on a banana plantation. It's boiling hot, and everyone's overworked. But I'm just determined to have a week's break at the coast at any rate. Don needs a break too—Dad and Mother can go away later.'

'Oh, Dad won't go,' said Don. 'He'll put up with the heat and take his holiday when there's not so much work on hand. Just now we've tons of fruit to pack and treat against fungus, and we have to put in a few more plants as well——'

'Banana growing, in fact,' remarked Sin for Eden's benefit, 'is a pretty tough form of agriculture and requires a lot of stamina. Well, you're pretty husky, Don. How's your father?'

'Twice as husky and healthy as I am,' said Don, and when he grinned as he did then his whole face changed, and Eden found herself thinking that maybe he would be lively enough for Amy after all. And better than a widower with an eight-year-old daughter. Though that was for Amy to say ...

Tea over, the question of whether or not Sin would come to the Websters for Christmas Day was reintroduced by Bibi.

'Please stay around till after Christmas, Sin. You can't spend the day on your own——'

'I have a married sister in Canberra, as a matter of fact,'

55

he told her with a smile, 'but we'll see what turns up. Thanks for thinking of me, anyhow.'

Soon after that he rose and said he must go. 'I have work to do.'

'I guess we'd better take off too,' said Bibi with a smile at Eden. 'We just came to introduce ourselves. Didn't expect the bonus of meeting up with you, though, Sin!'

'Our pleasure has been mutual,' he said agreeably, and Eden gritted her teeth. He certainly never talked to her that way—or looked at her like that either, though without being vain, she knew that she was prettier than Bibi. Though figurewise she didn't think she could compete.

At the door Don told Eden, 'We'll see you and Amy on Christmas Day, then. Come any time you like during the morning, and don't dress up too much, it's a bit oppressive up on the range—we miss out on the sea breeze.'

That night the telephone rang, and it was Amy.

'Eden? How's everything?'

'Fine,' said Eden. Khu Khan jumped on to her lap and began to purr. 'Was the party good? Are you still there or back at the flat?'

'It's all been super, and I'm still there. Tell me what's been happening.'

'Oh, nothing much.' After a second's consideration Eden decided not to mention Sinclair Watermount—he wasn't worth it, and anyhow, he would soon be off the scene. 'Khu Khan and I get along together really well. I've been swimming and I'm being terribly lazy. I love Christie's house—oh, and she left a great long message for you about the cat and the car and food and so on. And about a guy called Don Webster whom she wants you to meet.'

Amy laughed softly. 'Must be an old admirer. She was always trying to make me a gift of someone when she was in Brisbane. Have you met him yet?'

'Yes. He and his sister called in this afternoon to invite you to spend Christmas Day with the family. I got invited too and accepted for both of us.'

'Oh.' There was a short pause. 'Did you like him, Eden?'

'Me? He seemed very nice.'

'You can have him if you want him, Eden,' Amy interrupted. 'You'd be doing Christie a good turn—she does try to ease them off kindly, to introduce them to a new love object. You know why I'm not interested.'

Eden wasn't particularly interested either. Her pulse beat had stayed very steady when she'd met Don Webster, and she was positive, moreover, that the sight of her hadn't made his blood race either. It was absurd of Christie, and of Amy too, to try to parcel Don up and hand him to someone. She said equably, 'Well, we shan't fight over him, anyhow.'

'No.' There was another pause, and then Amy said with a rush, 'Eden—would you mind very much if I didn't come over for Christmas? You see, I've been asked to spend it with the Hewetts, and now I know you're all nicely fixed up I don't feel so bad about it. Of course I'll come on Tuesday if you really want me to——'

Eden's heart sank slightly. She *had* been looking forward to Amy's coming—and that wretched Watermount man had said he would stay till Amy came. But what sort of a friend would she be if she insisted that Amy should stick to their original arrangements just for her selfish reasons? Whatever reservations Eden had about the suitability of widowers, Amy was obviously madly in love with Malcolm Hewett, so——

'Amy,' she said lightly, 'you do whatever you like. I'm okay, and I certainly shan't be alone on Christmas Day.'

'Oh, good—you're a darling, Eden,' said Amy promptly. 'You'll probably find these Websters awfully hospitable. I wish you would fall for Don. Have fun, anyhow, won't you? Thanks again, and I'll see you after Christmas, that's a promise. I'll keep in touch.'

'Blow and damn,' thought Eden as she hung up. She stared across the room at Sin Watermount's portrait with narrowed eyes. Now he would dig in his toes and stay. But come to think of it, she didn't have to tell him that Amy had changed her plans. She wasn't obliged to pass on the latest news bulletin to him. She could, in fact, stick to the Tuesday story—make it Tuesday night, if she had to be definite. A little lie like that would do no one any harm. On the contrary, in fact. He would start off for Canberra on Tuesday—in the morning, she hoped—with an easy mind and the thought of duty done, and that would be that. Peace—freedom—for both of them.

One thing, though, she thought some time later as she prepared for bed. That bicycle he had offered her—that *would* be useful. She really didn't want to drive around in Christie's car, it was taking on a responsibility and she hadn't done a lot of driving. But neither was she keen on hoofing it in the heat every time she wanted to go shopping. Also, once Sin Watermount had gone, she would probably go to the lagoon to swim. She didn't fancy being drowned off Birrie Point.

She called in on him the following morning at about the time she calculated he would be having breakfast. The shell windbells by his door tinkled softly, the sunlight drifted dancingly through the jasmine vines, and shadows flickered on the pale uneven sandstone slabs of the patio floor. A handsome table made of heavy wooden planks straight from the bush was spread with a red-and-white checked cloth, so breakfast was imminent.

When he opened the door to her knock she had a glimpse of a big room floored with quarry tiles, and her nostrils caught the enticing aroma of fresh coffee and slightly burnt toast. He was wearing a midnight blue towelling robe and beneath it his legs looked muscly and brown. His hair was still damp and the whites of his eyes were slightly red from his early morning swim.

'Well?' he asked uncompromisingly.

'I came early so as not to disturb you once you start working,' she heard herself say just a little apologetically. 'I wondered if I might borrow your sister's bicycle after all. Please,' she added, and smiled—and knew as she did so that it was to hide her duplicity from him.

'Sure,' he said, 'sure.' He smiled back at her and she noticed how white his teeth were. 'It's in the garage—it's not locked up. Town? More shopping?'

She nodded and improvised. 'I want to make an early start, and look for some little gifts to take to the Websters.'

'Admirable,' he said dryly. 'Keep it as long as you like. There's no hurry with Lorraine away. House it up at Christie's if that suits you.'

'Thank you,' said Eden, and smiled again. Then as she was about to depart, he asked casually, 'You can't wait till Amy comes, is that it? I'd have thought you'd do better to go shopping for gifts together.'

She flushed guiltily. 'I—I thought I might collect a few ideas. It's hard when you don't know people.' She stopped because he was smiling quizzically.

'You don't have to think up excuses. I guess the money's burning a hole in your pocket now you've got the idea.'

'What money?' she flared, at once on the defensive.

He raised his brows. 'The money you want to spend, of course. Don't be so damned touchy. What money did you think I meant?'

'The money in the vase,' she said shortly. 'You did mean that. It would be typical of you to think I'd grab it——'

His green eyes looked at her ruefully. 'We started off well this morning. It's a pity we can't come to terms with each other.'

59

Eden shrugged, a little disarmed but not trusting him. 'Does it matter? You'll be leaving in the morning—to-morrow, I mean,' she amended it hastily. 'It's Tuesday—Amy will—should be here.'

'So she should,' he agreed. He gestured towards the table. 'Will you join me for coffee? Or have you break-fasted already?'

'I've breakfasted,' she lied, and thought wearily that she was becoming too adept lately at playing around with the truth. It appeared there was something in the saying about giving a dog a bad name ... She half turned away. 'I hope you hunt up all the information you want in Canberra. And—and I suppose I should wish you a happy Christmas, in case I don't see you before you leave.'

'Oh, you'll see me, Eden. I shall make a point of calling to see that you aren't in any strife. And to say goodbye.'

Eden managed a wretched smile.

She found the bicycle and rode it back to Christie's. The thought that she was in possession of it gave her a feeling of freedom and independence, and she decided she would have a day out. It would reduce the likelihood of Sin find-ing out about Amy, anyhow, if she wasn't around. She didn't feel like swimming at Birrie Beach. The waves looked enormous and she wasn't reassured by the fact that he had taken his morning dip as usual. He would quite likely be only too pleased if she did drown herself—or half drown herself anyway, she amended it, picturing him coming to her rescue and giving her a good talking-to before she had halfway recovered.

She took care over the locking up, then set off on the bicycle for the lagoon. There she wallowed lazily in the sun-warmed water, then lay on the sand listening to the drowsy sound of the cicadas singing away the hot summer day, and watching the children sliding down the sandhills or chasing each other through the tea trees and the tangle of lantana that grew on the landward side of the lagoon. She had brought fruit with her, and that served for lunch. She could have got herself a boy-friend several times over if she'd wanted, but she ignored the suntanned young men in trunks who loitered in her vicinity, and eventually joined a couple of children who were building an elaborate system of dams.

By the time she'd cycled into town and made a few necessary purchases, Eden was feeling so drugged with sun and salt and sea air that all she wanted was a sound sleep.

So passed Monday, and when she was ready for bed she took a last look through the bush at the lights shining from Sin Watermount's bungalow and hoped it would be in darkness the following night.

In the morning she went nervily down to the beach for a swim. The sea looked so flat and quiet, she calculated it must be one of the good days. Sin Watermount, she hoped, was in his bungalow packing up. But when she reached the beach she saw that he was out on the rocks at the far end, fishing. The tide was high and the water came swirling in almost quietly over the rocks, so he was in water up to his thighs. He stood statue-like, his bronzed torso gilded by the sun, and Eden watched him uneasily. Was he really fishing? Or was he thinking? She supposed even writers must have problems occasionally, and somehow he looked so remote and withdrawn that she didn't want to disturb him.

All the same she walked slowly over the beach towards the rather flat surf. It was then that she saw something written in the sand just beyond the reach of the waves.

Danger. Keep Out.

Danger? With the sea quiet like that? He was just trying to frighten her away, to keep the beach to himself. So what was she going to do? Reluctantly, she admitted to herself that she'd be a fool to ignore the warning. It just might be genuine. And then if she got into difficulties, he'd be within his rights to be angry.

So okay, she'd forgo the swim. As for sunbathing, he couldn't forbid her the use of the sand. But no, she thought after a moment, she wouldn't be able to relax knowing he was there on the rocks and likely to come and disturb her at any time he chose. He might even question her about Amy, and she didn't know whether she would be able to hold out or if she might weaken and tell him the truth.

She turned away, and slowly and cautiously retraced her footsteps till she reached the beginning of the narrow path up the cliff.

Back at the bungalow, she pulled on jeans and shirt over her swimsuit and cycled off to the lagoon.

She saw nothing of Sin when she went home that evening, and when darkness came and she looked through the window at the lights that had begun to show from the distant shore, there was no sign of life at his bungalow.

Relieved, yet somehow incredulous, she checked up every half-hour or so, but she was right, and there was still no sign that he was home when she went to bed.

'So he's gone,' she thought, switching out her light. Her feeling of triumph, of having got the better of him, was oddly confused with some other indefinable feeling. She wished Amy really would be arriving late tonight or some time tomorrow. It was going to be kind of lonely here with only Khu Khan, who at that moment sprang lightly on to her bed, to keep her company.

CHAPTER FOUR

WHEN she woke in the morning it was to an acute awareness of the fact that Sin Watermount had gone. Their
association had come to an end, and that was what she had
been wishing for ever since she came to the coast. He
wouldn't be swimming out beyond the breakers today or
writing messages in the sand for her. The beach was all
hers. If she wanted to take chances with Birrie Beach, then
it was up to her, and if it pleased her, *she* could be the one
who was down there at six o'clock in the morning.

Eden glanced at the digital clock on the bedside table. It
was three minutes past six now. She scrambled out of bed,
let Khu Khan out of the front door, then looked over to
the sea to check that he wasn't there. And of course he
wasn't. He must be well on the way to Canberra, she
thought. She found her swimming gear and got into it,
took up her surf towel and with a secret little feeling of
trepidation, made for the beach.

She jumped the last few feet down on to the soft white
sand and then stopped dead. She couldn't believe it! Not
ten feet away stood Sin Watermount, his tanned torso
gleaming above his swimming trunks. He was smoking and
his back was towards her, and he stood in an attitude that
she instinctively read as one of deep thought.

So he had merely been out last night, that was all, and
while she was deeply and peacefully asleep he had returned.

'Damn!' thought Eden. Yet her heart had begun to beat
fast, and she was aware of a peculiar feeling that was almost
—pleasure.

63

She about-faced, and very quietly began to clamber on to the path again.

His voice stopped her.

'Hello there! What's the trouble? Changed your mind about a swim?'

She turned guiltily. 'I—I didn't know you were here. I thought you'd gone—I——'

He tossed down his cigarette. 'Oh, come on now—I told you I'd be over to say goodbye before I left. And I don't own the beach, you know . . . Did Amy arrive safely?'

'Er—no—not yet,' she floundered, her cheeks crimsoning.

He frowned, and his green-eyed glance sharpened. 'She was expected yesterday, wasn't she? Did you have any word she'd changed her plans?'

Eden bit her lip, and began to wish she had told the truth to begin with. 'Yes,' she admitted reluctantly. 'She—she couldn't get away yesterday after all.'

He looked at her in silence for a moment and she dreaded his next probing question, but all he asked was, 'When, then?'

Eden dropped her beach towel and stooped to pick it up, hoping to hide her guilty face and pink cheeks.

'Well?' he said. 'Today? Tomorrow?'

Put on the spot like that, she couldn't do anything but tell the truth, and she did so with a wry grimace. 'She won't be here till after Christmas is over, if you want to know.'

'Certainly I want to know,' he said with a lift of his brows.

'Don't let it interfere with your plans, anyhow,' Eden said brightly, tossing back her hair.

Sin studied her for an instant and then he said, 'Are you coming into the water?' and with that he turned his back and without waiting for an answer, strode in the direction of the surf.

Eden stood undecided. But it would be stupid not to go in, now she was here. The day was young and beautiful, the water sparkled and the sky was cloudless. Moreover, she had a protector. What more could any girl ask?

Sin had plunged beneath the breakers, and she watched him swim out beyond the line of foam, into the rocking, jewel-blue depths where he would take his morning exercise. It must be wonderful to swim out there, to feel powerful enough to hold your own with the Pacific Ocean as it came rolling in past Danger Point.

Eden ran across the sand, and in a few seconds she too had plunged into the heart of a green wave that came dashing shorewards to embrace the white sands. But that was as far as she followed Sin. The deep water was not for her, and she contented herself staying well within her depth and meeting the challenge of the waves in her own way. She felt utterly exhilarated, and she had lost completely that feeling that coming to Australia had been a disaster. Life was pretty good—despite Sin Watermount.

She left the sea before he did and went back to the bungalow where she showered and dressed, then breakfasted with appetite. She was outside in the shade giving Khu Khan a good brushing, which he loved, when Sin appeared with a polythene-wrapped parcel.

'Fish,' he said briefly, 'I caught it yesterday. I came to see if you'd like some, but you were out. You might spare a bit for the animal too, he's very partial to fish.'

He smiled and Eden accepted the parcel with surprise. So he thought of Christie's 'animal' in a kindly way sometimes, did he? She had formed the impression that he had no time for Khu at all. She took the fish and thanked him, and he asked quizzically, 'I suppose you know how to cook it?'

Her head went up and there was a quick retort ready on her lips. Did he think she was completely stupid and useless? But before the words were out she held them back, reflecting ruefully that it had become quite a habit with her to be rude and sharp-tongued. Not a very gracious way to receive a gift! And he probably didn't mean any harm by his question. She said meekly, 'Yes, I do. I'm quite good with fish. And—and thank you very much.'

'Think nothing of it.' His white teeth flashed in a pleasant smile as he turned and left her.

'Well, what do you know?' she asked Khu Khan, who was rolling about at her feet virtually asking for his grooming to continue. 'He doesn't really dislike little pusscats after all—you're to have fish for your dinner tonight.'

The small incident affected Eden sufficiently for her to be aware of a definite, but somewhat cautious, change in her feeling towards Sin Watermount. He wasn't altogether unbearable. He was often hard and unnecessarily condemnatory, and through no fault of her own she had started off on the wrong foot with him. But it didn't help matters for her to be rude and touchy, and she had to admit to herself she had been, and as from now she was going to remedy that. He would soon see that she wasn't such a bad sort of a girl, and as it looked as though she was going to have to suffer his presence for a few more days anyhow, that might not be a bad thing.

'And let's face it,' she reminded herself next afternoon as she prepared to cycle in to town, 'it *is* reassuring to have someone about the place.'

She hadn't encountered him since he had brought the fish, and it was almost as if they had been avoiding each other, so she was taken by surprise as she rode slowly down the drive to see him coming through the banksias from next door. The rate of Eden's heartbeat increased just a little and a slight flush rose to her cheeks as she slowed down her pace still more. Before today, she would quite likely have pretended not to see him and pedalled as fast as she could, but today was different—though she soon discovered that resolutions are easy to make and difficult to stick to.

The sun shone on his hair, making the bleached streaks look golden, and the definite and uncompromising lines of his very masculine face were emphasised by the strong light that produced equally strong shadows. She thought, not for the first time, 'No, he's not exactly handsome'. Yet there was something forceful and even impressive about Sin's face and his whole bearing. She would even admit that it was not impossible to imagine Christie Vaughan might be madly in love with him—though he was certainly no dreamboat as far as Eden Dare was concerned ...

'Where are you off to?' he asked. And automatically she felt her hackles rise. He wasn't asking, he was *demanding*, and her brand-new feelings of tolerance drooped somewhat. The very way he was looking at her was enough to make her feel aggressive.

'Shopping,' she said curtly. 'And I've locked the house —both doors and all the windows. If you want to do an inspection, you know where the key is.' Her voice faded a little with the last few words. Already she was thinking despairingly, 'Now why on earth did I say all that?' The bicycle wavered and she was forced to slip to the ground, and found herself just too close to him with those green, enigmatic eyes looking at her sardonically.

'It's not my habit to operate behind anyone's back,' he said sharply.

She bit her lip in vexation. That, as sure as her name was Eden Dare, was a reference to her own supposedly underhand 'operations' when her grandfather was away. So what was the use of her making resolutions to be easy to get on with if he was going to hold *that* against her?

'No?' she queried, her chin up. 'What about the other day when you were prowling around trying all the doors?'

He gave a tight smile. 'Was that an inspection? You didn't come out of it very well, at any rate. However, I simply came to let you know that I've just been on the phone to the Websters. As you hadn't let them know of Amy's change of plans I did so for you, and took up the invitation they gave me the other day. I shan't be leaving here yet ... I thought you might like to know you can come in my car to Nepelle Heights on Christmas Day. I'll let you know later what time I plan to leave.'

Eden's cheeks burned. Was that or was it not a rap over the knuckles for bad manners in not letting the Websters know about Amy? She managed a casual smile and told him, 'You didn't need to act on my behalf. I'd have let the Websters know what was happening in good time and—and I'd planned to take a taxi,' she improvised.

'On Christmas morning? You'd be lucky. There's a dearth of taxis in this town. And it's not safe for a girl like you to try hitch-hiking, if you should start thinking along those lines.'

'Don't worry, I won't,' she retorted, mounting the bicycle again. She rode off quickly without mentioning his offer of a lift but knowing she would have to accept it, and feeling increasingly ashamed of her rudeness as she cycled along.

Perhaps it was partly to atone for that rudeness that when she bought some gifts in the town, she included a tie for him—rather expensive and rather distinctive, and he probably wouldn't like it. She bought handmade chocolates for Mrs Webster, a big jar of nuts for Mr Webster, some scented soap for Bibi, and a tie for Don—younger-looking and less exclusive than the one for Sin. She came out of it with her meagre savings somewhat diminished, but feeling quite cheerful. Amy would come, and back in Kamballa she'd find work, and she wasn't worrying.

Her rudeness to Sin Watermount continued to prey on Eden's mind, and the following day she forced herself to go to his door, thank him for his offer to take her to Nepelle Heights, and accept gracefully. Nevertheless she had the impression she had interrupted his work, and the minute she had said her piece she flitted off.

Sin didn't bother her after that, he didn't even call to make final arrangements for Christmas, he merely rang her.

'Eleven o'clock,' he told her. 'That should give you ample time to make yourself look pretty.'

Finally she found she was looking forward to it. She was lonely. She thought back to Christmas last year—the last Christmas she had spent with her mother. It hadn't been terribly festive, because her mother was a semi-invalid by that time, but at least they had been together. Neither of them had had an inkling that twelve months later everything would have altered drastically, though perhaps in retrospect, her mother might have suspected it. Aunt Sylvia had sent a warm and loving card, and Eden's mother had said on a sigh, 'Poor Sylvia! I often wish we hadn't lost touch as much as we have. It would be wonderful to see her again—but one shouldn't ask the impossible.'

Eden didn't take a swim on Christmas morning, though *he* did. She had breakfast, then showered and washed her hair, and while it was drying flicked around with a duster, as Sin Watermount had put it. She had almost an hour to wait before he would arrive, and after she had done some general dusting, she dusted each small ornament in turn. There were animals of all kinds and sizes in glass and ceramics and even in bronze, and several elegant figurines of various sizes, some of them, she was certain, quite valuable, though she didn't know enough to recognise an antique for sure. One piece, a delicately tinted figure of a girl with a cat, was really exquisite, and she took it over to the window to admire it. As she turned it carefully in her hands, she could see that it had been broken and mended. The head, in fact, must have been broken off, for she could see the line where the two pieces had been put together again.

Her nerves jumped suddenly as the doorbell rang loudly and imperiously, and to her dismay, the ornament slipped from her hands. Although it fell on the soft pale green rug, it broke—or at least, the head came off again, and she stooped and picked it up as she went to the door, Khu Khan twining himself about her legs.

It was Sin Watermount—who else?—and Eden exclaimed, 'You're early! I'm not quite ready.'

'So I see.' He was looking at the broken ornament she held, and she coloured guiltily. Oh God, was she going to be in trouble now for smashing up Christie's precious ornaments? She supposed so, for though Sin said nothing, he looked at her in an accusing way, a way that made his displeasure very plain. One would have thought the thing belonged to him, and although she was inclined to accept that most of the contents of the bungalow had once belonged to William Vaughan, who knew? It would be just her luck if Sin had given this particular object to Christie. He had followed her into the house and she put the pieces carefully on a table, then stooped and picked up Khu Khan, and held him like a woman protecting herself with a child.

Sin said dryly, 'Don't tell me the cat's to blame. Christie claims her animal's faultless when it comes to dodging obstacles on shelves and table tops.'

Eden bit her lip. It hadn't occurred to her to blame the *animal*, and she said at once, 'I'm not blaming Khu Khan.'

His eyebrows rose. 'What, then? The wind blowing the curtains into the room knocked the thing over?'

'I dropped it,' she said, coldly angry at being expected to tell lies to excuse herself. 'I was—flicking around with a duster.' She added with perfect truth, though she realised at once she would have done better to have held her tongue, 'If you want to know, my nerves jumped when you rang the bell—so loudly and so early. Half an hour before the time you said you'd come. But I suppose you won't believe that. You'd prefer to think I've started deliberately smashing Christie's treasures to bits.'

'Don't be absurd,' he interrupted her sharply. 'Of course I know it must have been an accident. But in future forget the dusting. You don't have to indulge in that sort of thing simply to prove me wrong. And don't expect me to be entirely complacent about your carelessness either ... now I suggest you run along and finish dressing.'

Exasperated, Eden turned her back and went to her bedroom. Had she been careless? She supposed so. Yet if it hadn't been broken before—— She sighed. It was no use speculating. But what a rotten start to the day!

When she rejoined Sin several minutes later her hair was shining and groomed, and she was dressed coolly in a sleeveless dress of fine soft cotton in ivory and pale violet, and she carried her prettily-wrapped gifts in a small shopping basket she had found in the kitchen.

Sin said at once, as though he had made up his mind to do so, 'Okay, Eden—I accept that what happened was an accident and we'll forget it. I got carried away a little because that figure is something that Christie prizes rather specially.'

She looked at him without speaking for a moment. Christie had prized it, yet she—or someone—had broken it, and mended it. Well, it wasn't for her to tell him that if he didn't already know.

71

'I'll mend it, of course,' she said.

He shrugged. 'You'd better leave it alone. It's lost its value now.'

She repeated, 'I'll mend it. Now, can we go?'

They went. And despite everything, Eden soon found she was enjoying the long drive up into the ranges and the spectacular view back to the coast where the turquoise ocean, streaked with emerald in the shallows, shimmered and shone as beautiful as a dream. Soon they were on steep slopes with acre upon acre of banana plantations, all entrancingly green, and looking about her with delight Eden was scarcely aware of the increasing humidity. She forgot her feud with Sin too, as he talked interestingly about the countryside, and told her that she and Amy would have to take a picnic up to the Big Scrub—the rain-forest of the north coast.

'You can swim in the river pools and take a look at the birds and the plant life peculiar to that area—if such things interest you.'

'They do,' she assured him, and then they reached the turn-off to Nepelle Heights plantation. The Websters had about eight acres of bananas, he told her, and among the broad green banner-like leaves on the hillsides she could see great bunches of the yellowing fruit, with here and there the gleam of red or blue or yellow—the plastic covers used to protect the ripening bananas from the climate. When she exclaimed in surprise at seeing irrigation pipes, he told her, 'Bananas need at least an inch of rain every week all year round, and irrigating is a sure way of seeing they get it.'

As they drove up to the Websters' house, high on the slopes, he pointed out the big packing shed and the wires radiating out from it to every part of the plantation— 'flying foxes', used to carry down the heavy bunches of bananas. In the packing shed, the bananas had to be dehanded and packed, and the boxes dipped in fungicide before being sent off to the markets.

Mr and Mrs Webster were simple people, very Australian and obviously hard-working. Mr Webster was lean with a tanned and leathery face, his wife was overweight, slightly harassed-looking and flushed from the heat. They made the visitors welcome, and Eden explained that Amy had been invited to spend Christmas with friends and would be at Burrangarra in a day or two. Iced beer was produced —and Eden, although she didn't care for beer, drank a glass just to be sociable. She had the feeling Bibi would think her a snob if she refused, but she found she needed to dip into the savouries fairly frequently to make the beer supportable.

After some time she rather uncertainly produced her gifts, and Sin too handed round small packages, one of them for Eden. Mrs Webster was delighted with her chocolates, kissed Eden and said, 'That's sweet of you, love,' then opened the box and passed it round immediately. Mr Webster declared his jar of nuts to be 'beaut', Don admired his tie and Bibi sniffed her soap and said it was exotic. Eden hardly liked to look at Sin as he unwrapped his tie. She wished nervously that she had chosen something less obviously expensive, and couldn't imagine now what had got into her. Certainly he seemed surprised and pleased as well, but Bibi widened her eyes and gave a low whistle as she hung on Sin's arm rather possessively and watched. She raised her brows at Eden and remarked, not very politely, 'That must have cost you something! Are you made of money—just like Christie?'

Eden hid her embarrassment—and annoyance—by opening the gift Sin had given her. It was a beautiful square of Thai silk in two shades of violet that by some coincidence toned exactly with the dress she was wearing. Bibi, she saw, had received a similar square, but hers was of a rich

73

golden yellow, and she went at once to a gilt-framed mirror on the wall and knotted it around her neck, then turned to Sin for his admiration, her brown eyes alight. Her thanks were fulsome and she flung her arms around Sin's neck to kiss him, behaviour which he accepted without turning a hair. When in the midst of her rapture Bibi happened to glance round and see that Eden too had received a scarf, her face fell rather comically. Had she thought Sin's gift to her was personal and special? Eden wondered wryly. If he was engaged, that would hardly be likely ...

Nevertheless Bibi and Sin disappeared outside shortly after, and Eden went to help Mrs Webster carry in the cold dinner—great platters of turkey and ham and pork decorated with parsley and sliced cucumber, and several bowls of different salads, all very beautifully set out and enticing. It was a buffet lunch, and the table in the not-very-large dining room was crowded with enough food for twenty, Eden thought, for there were dishes of olives and gherkins and pickled onions, of nuts and sweets and crystallised fruits as well. The pudding was a dream, and altogether Eden's favourite part of the meal—tropical fruits mixed with marshmallows and sour cream, delicately flavoured with ginger and served with scoops of frozen vanilla mousse. To her relief there was no more beer, but fruit punch followed later by a much-needed cup of coffee.

The rest of the afternoon passed lazily. Eden helped Mrs Webster do the washing up in the hot kitchen while the three men and Bibi went to the sitting room where the big ceiling fan was whirring. When Eden went to join them, Bibi was sitting on the arm of Sin's chair, one long leg swinging, a dish of macadamia nuts in her hand and her mouth full. Eden thought a little unkindly that if she didn't watch it she would soon be as overweight as her mother, though to be truthful there was no sign of that happening, for while she had a full bosom, her waist was very trim indeed. All the same the macadamia nuts, though delicious, were very rich and oily, and Eden found two or three quite enough for her—particularly after a large meal.

There was a thunderstorm late in the afternoon, and it was a thrill to watch the rain come sweeping in from away out over the sea, to envelop the ranges and beat against that other sea of bright green leaves. The temperature dropped as the rain drummed deafeningly on the iron roof, and the broad green leaves bent and swayed and surged about. Then quite suddenly it was all over, the sun came out, the earth steamed, birds called and three black swans, their long necks outstretched, flew across the sky uttering their harsh honking cry.

Sin and Eden stayed to tea, though Eden at any rate had no appetite, for she felt she had done nothing but eat and drink all day. When at last they drove off in the car, with Bibi's cry of 'see you!' ringing in their ears, she leaned back exhausted on the seat into a silence that was strangely comfortable—as if she and Sin were going home together.

'To an empty house and to poor Khu Khan, Eden Dare,' she corrected herself mentally.

'Poor Khu!' she exclaimed aloud as at last they drove along by the lagoon where the lights of prawning holiday-makers glimmered eerily in the warm night. 'He'll be so hungry—he'll think I've deserted him——'

'Now, Eden,' Sin's voice was half amused, half aggravated. 'Don't get maudlin—you wouldn't have had me leave straight after tea so you could come home and feed the cat. He can wait. He'll appreciate his meal—and you—all the more for it. That's how it is in life—you don't appreciate what comes too easily.'

'Philosophising,' thought Eden tiredly. But, 'I suppose you're right,' she agreed. 'He *will* be pleased to see me.'

As he leaned across to open the door for her when they reached the bungalow he said seriously, 'It was generous of you to buy me such a splendid gift, Eden.' For an instant she wondered if there was a touch of cynicism in his tone—if he imagined she had rifled the Chinese vase—but it was a thought unworthy of Christmas and she stifled it and said graciously, 'I'm glad if you really liked it. My mother always said ties are difficult to choose.'

'Well, you judged my taste exactly,' he assured her. 'I couldn't be more pleased.'

'And my scarf,' she said a little shyly. 'Violet's one of my favourite colours.'

They smiled at each other for what seemed a long moment and then, unnerved, she said a quick goodnight and climbed out of the car and ran to find Khu Khan. Sin Watermount looked so different when he smiled at her in the starlight—his eyes softened by shadows, the white of his teeth gleaming faintly—the hardness, the disapproval, the cynicism gone ...

Well, Christmas Day was over now, the truce would be called off, and everything would revert to normal—she would, as Amy had put it, turn into a pumpkin again.

And sure enough, she spent the next day completely alone. The most exciting thing she did was to mend the broken figure with some glue she found in a drawer in the kitchen.

Christie at any rate wouldn't see any difference, she thought, when she had finished. But Sin, if he saw that thin line around the girl's neck, would think of Eden Dare and her carelessness. And that was probably the only time he would think of her.

CHAPTER FIVE

THE telephone rang that night just as Eden was about to call Khu Khan inside, and she flew to answer it, knowing it must be Amy with news that she would be arriving, Eden hoped, tomorrow.

But Amy was not arriving tomorrow.

She was all apologies for not being in touch sooner— 'Did you have a marvellous Christmas? Oh, I did, it was just brilliant. I'm back at the flat now, and——'

She paused and Eden put in eagerly, 'Are you coming over tomorrow? It will be lovely to see you——'

'Oh, Eden,' Amy groaned, 'I'm in such a predicament, and I'm so ashamed of leaning on you like this, but here we go again! Malc is taking his holidays now, it's the only time of year when things are quiet enough. He has a cottage on the coast south of Coffs, and he wants me to come with them. A little friend of Barbie's has been invited too, and it should be really fun. I'm afraid I've said yes, but of course I won't go if you really want me there.'

As she listened to her, Eden's heart sank. So she was to continue being a stone around Sin Watermount's neck, because he'd made up his mind not to go until Amy came, which was absurd—but try and tell him that! What a drag for him—and what a pain in the neck for her. Rapidly, she wondered if she could lie to him again and pretend that Amy was coming. But it wouldn't work—she knew that. He just didn't trust her an inch ...

Even while her mind was juggling with these problems, she was telling Amy, 'Of course you mustn't change your plans on my account! Only, Amy, don't you think you should be a bit weary? I mean, this man's a widower—mightn't he be more interested in getting someone to look after Barbie, rather than a wife? Widowers do have a reputation for looking for housekeepers, and you're only young——'

'Eden!' Amy interrupted, and actually laughed. 'Malc is thirty-one. He's not in his dotage. He already has a housekeeper, and she'll be coming to the coast with us, she's a darling. Malc and I are madly in love with each other. He hasn't actually asked me to marry him yet, but he will—even if I don't take this holiday with him. But it would help us to get to know each other better.'

'Oh,' said Eden inadequately. 'Well, of course you must go. I wouldn't stop you for the world.'

'I know you wouldn't. You're a real pal,' Amy said gratefully. 'I hope you're not having a dull time and aren't frightened on your own. It's a lonely spot.'

'No, I'm not frightened. Sinclair Watermount is next door anyhow,' Eden confessed resignedly, more to set Amy's mind at rest than for any other reason.

'*What?* He didn't go to Bangkok? Why on earth not? Christie didn't say a word—and I haven't heard from her yet, though I've written to let her know about you.'

'He must have pulled out at the last moment,' Eden said briefly. 'He had some extra work to do on this book he was writing, something like that.'

'What a shame. Poor old Christie ... Do you like him, Eden? He's super, isn't he?'

'I don't see much of him,' Eden said evasively. 'He's working most of the time.'

'Oh, I suppose so. But at least he's there ... Anyhow, thanks again, Eden, for being such a pet. Be seeing you.'

They said goodbye and Eden hung up. So Mafeking was not to be relieved—not for how long? Well, she would sleep

78

on it, she thought with a grimace. Maybe Sin Watermount would have to go to Canberra regardless, and maybe some bright idea would come to her as to how to handle the situation overnight.

Meanwhile, she suddenly realised that a tropical downpour was in progress and that Khu Khan was still outside. It was a wonder he wasn't scratching at the door or tapping on the windowpane wanting to be let in. He was really a very intelligent creature. She opened the front door hopefully, but there was no blue-eyed Siamese cat with a drenched fur coat cowering outside. She flicked on the garden light and called him several times, but he didn't appear.

Bother! She would have to get hold of him. It was getting late and she wasn't going to stay up all night. Impulsively, she began to hurry down the path, calling the cat and pausing to listen for the sound of his almost human voice. Quite suddenly he darted out of a thick clump of bushes, but before she could pounce on him he flitted across the path and disappeared again. Wretched creature! Why didn't he head for home? Eden glimpsed him again and followed exasperatedly, uncomfortable now in her soaking clothes, and pushing her wet hair out of her eyes. He was heading straight for Sin Watermount's bungalow, from which a light shone, dancingly visible through the slanting rain.

The cat leaped like an imp through the wet bushes, and Eden followed, aware of the scent of ginger blossoms heavy on the air. To her exasperation Christie's treasured animal shinned up a banksia tree that grew close to the house near the lighted window, and she paused for a moment, reluctant to follow him now, or to call out. The rain eased off momentarily, and in the comparative silence she could hear the uneasy roar and rush of the sea as it surged over the sand on the beach below. A brilliant shaft of moonlight struck through a narrow gap in the clouds so that they were deckle-edged in sharp gold. Eden blinked the raindrops from her lashes and moved quietly forward.

'Khu Khan darling,' she called softly, 'come on down, there's a good pussy!'

The cat, perched on a branch almost level with the room, tilted his head at her and swished his tail playfully.

'Come down at once!' she repeated, sternly now, and moved closer. Through the lighted window she glimpsed Sin Watermount sitting at his typewriter, but thank heavens, his back was towards her, and with sudden determination she dashed forward. The next instant she had tripped and knocked something flying with an unholy clatter. She managed to save herself from sprawling on her face by grabbing at the banksia tree.

Well, her number was up now. She would be in trouble again, and it would be no use to turn and flee. Besides, she wasn't going home without the cat, who had now sprung on to the roof where he crouched as if to discover what was going on below.

An outside light went on and Eden was revealed in all her splendour, looking, she supposed, like a drowned rat, and Sin Watermount's voice exclaimed exasperatedly, 'It's you, is it, Eden Dare? What in hell are you doing now, crashing around in the dark? If you want something, why can't you come to the door and ring the bell like a normal human being? Have you locked yourself out, for God's sake?' And his green eyes took in her drenched form, clad in jeans and shirt that fitted her like a second, though wrinkled, skin.

'I'm sorry about the clatter,' she said stiffly. 'I didn't mean to disturb you, I tripped over something accidentally. I was—I was trying to get hold of Khu Khan before I go to bed.' She stooped to right the object that had tripped her, and discovered it was a terracotta pot—broken now, of course, and the soil it contained scattered about. But the plant wasn't broken, and what was a pot when it could have been an antique or something?

'Leave it,' ordered Sin impatiently, and added, 'That damned animal! Where is it?'

'*He*'s on the roof,' said Eden coldly, but when she looked Khu Khan was not there. 'Well, he was,' she defended herself, 'till you came out and frightened him away.'

'I should imagine *you* were the one who frightened him away,' he countered, and for an instant they stared at each other. 'Well, get along and find the cat before we have another downpour and I'm stuck with you. Complete your mission and take yourself home to bed, and quit making the night hideous with your racket. I suppose it hasn't occurred to you that I chose this place to work because of the peace and quiet—which has vanished completely since you came.' Eden opened her mouth ready for an angry retort, but he swept on, 'Isn't it enough that I have you on my mind all day without extending your influence into the night?'

Okay, she thought, so she had made a row tonight. But she didn't disturb him during the day. She told him remotely, 'You should have gone to Canberra and done your research, shouldn't you?'

He raised his brows. 'I'm not leaving you here on your own,' he stated categorically.

Eden felt sick. He would kill her if he knew that Amy wasn't coming for another two weeks or so. She bit her lip and turned away to look for Khu Khan. 'You can go back to your work now, anyhow,' she told Sin. 'I shan't make another sound—not if I have to tiptoe round silently searching till morning.'

He laughed mirthlessly. 'You won't do that—not on any cat's behalf. However, I'll give you a hand. If you were a friend of Christie's you'd know that her animal comes to a whistle, just like a dog. The Siamese is no ordinary feline.'

He proceeded to demonstrate, and within half a minute the cat was there. Eden picked him up. 'It's a pity you didn't tell me that days ago, then I shouldn't have disturbed you tonight. Well, it won't happen again. Goodnight.'

'Goodnight,' he answered shortly, and they parted company.

Eden worried about the situation before she fell asleep. She was sorry she had interrupted his work, but it was just one of those accidents that simply happen. She hadn't been to blame. If only he would trust her and go away, they would both be happy. As it was, she still had to break the news to him that Amy's arrival had been deferred again, but she was quite determined that somehow she was going to convince him that he didn't need to stay around. The only possible thing to do, it seemed to her, was to make a clean breast of everything, tell him the whole truth about Berry and that business at Overlooking so that he would see he had based his assessment of her character on a wrong premise. He mightn't believe her, of course, but at least she could try. Once she had made up her mind about this, she fell asleep deeply and peacefully.

She rose early in the morning, let Khu Khan out, and checked that Sin was having his swim. Then she made herself coffee, showered and dressed carefully. She was going to make a good impression this morning, and she chose a sleeveless, rose-coloured cotton dress with a flared skirt and a wide belt. She brushed her darker-than-blonde hair till it was gleaming and let it fall neatly against her cheeks. Her freckles were fading into the healthy suntan she had acquired, and the clear grey of her eyes was intensified by the contrast with her tanned skin. She used a little moisturising cream and a touch of lipstick, and glanced at the digital clock. Sin should be having his breakfast now, out on the patio. She would beard him there, as it were. He couldn't complain she was interrupting his work if he hadn't yet begun it. She would put the record straight, apologise for being a disruptive influence, and appeal to him to do her the courtesy of trusting her. Yes, she would lay her cards on the table. She would be frank and honest and adult ...

It was not, of course, the piece of cake she had persuaded herself it would be. To begin with, she had to wait a full sixty seconds before he answered the doorbell, and she knew the minute he opened the door that she had disturbed him in the shower. His thick hair was wet and towel-ruffled, and he wore a longish dark blue towelling robe. His eyes looked blue-green this morning, and he raised dark eyebrows and asked her flatly,

'Well? Is it something urgent? I've barely finished showering and I haven't breakfasted yet.'

Eden flushed uncomfortably crimson. Those searching, suspicious eyes flicked over her pretty dress, her off-white sandals, the whole of her meticulous appearance. 'What on earth does he think I want?' she wondered, and before she could speak he answered her thoughts by suggesting, 'I take it you're gallivanting off somewhere for the day and want some kind of favour.'

She shook her head, suddenly tongue-tied. It wasn't easy to explain what she *did* want.

'No, I—please don't let me stop you from getting your breakfast. I—there were—just some things I wanted to explain—to—to straighten out.'

He frowned and said resignedly, 'Come on in then, and get it off your mind. Have you eaten yet?'

'Er—yes,' she said, not quite truthfully, as she had had only coffee. She stepped inside feeling a mass of nerves. It was so easy to think of yourself putting your side of the question, but quite different when it came to the point. She followed him through to the kitchen, noticing with half her mind as they passed through the living room the hexagonal terracotta floor tiles, some hand-worked tapestries on the wall, chairs and sofa in black leather, and a fascinating coffee table of smoked glass supported by two crouching figures, either sculptured in stone or cast from cement.

The kitchen was modern, but had an air of comfort as well, and around the small breakfast nook was a rather lush wallpaper in rich blues and green. A little awkwardly Eden took a chair at the small table, while Sin started the coffee percolating and put bacon in a pan. About to take eggs from the fridge, he turned and asked her quizzically, 'Sure you won't join me?'

'I'll—I'll have some coffee, then,' she said nervously. 'It smells good.'

He smiled slightly. 'I think you have a lean and hungry look—I don't believe you've eaten. And you can't be weight-watching with that svelte figure. I'll fry you an egg too, and here—you can make some toast while you get your tongue untied. I've never known you so reticent. You've got me on edge wondering what I'm about to hear. Let's hope it's not some new and tragic disaster at the bungalow next door.'

That stirred her temper slightly.

'There haven't been any disasters next door,' she retorted, 'at least not while I've been there. You always seem to expect the worst, and that's what I want to straighten out.' She bent her head over the platter of sliced wholemeal bread he had set on the table and loaded a couple of pieces into the pop-up toaster.

'Carry on,' he said offhandedly.

She groped for words to start, then plunged in desperately. 'I know you think it's a pain in the neck that I came here instead of Amy, but that's only because you got the

84

wrong idea about me that day at Overlooking.' She put right out of her head the memory of how he had caught her looking through his windows, and hoped that *he* wasn't remembering it at this instant.

'I did? And you aim to put me right?'

She nodded and stared at his unco-operative back as he turned to manipulate the bacon.

'Yes. I suppose you think I was given no responsibilities at the gallery because I wasn't trustworthy, but that's not true. I was sort of on trial—to see how much Pomeroy blood ran in my veins,' she added, her voice unconsciously ironical. 'In the meantime, I did the cooking and the house-keeping, and occasionally a little of the bookwork—all the things Aunt Sylvia used to do.'

She paused and Sin broke eggs into the pan, four of them, and prompted her, 'Your aunt's not there now?'

'No. She died before I got here. You see, when I lost my mother back home in England, Aunt Sylvia wrote and asked me to come and live with her and my grandfather. I think she was lonely, and she really wanted me. I thought I'd be able to work in Kamballa and—oh, take up something I was interested in in my spare time, perhaps. I never had time at home, my mother wasn't well, and as soon as I left school I had to take over the handicrafts shop.'

She stopped to butter the toast and made a little face. She wasn't getting anywhere with what she had meant to say, babbling on aimlessly about things that weren't really relevant. He must be bored stiff.

'Well, carry on,' he encouraged her, ladling a large rasher of bacon and two eggs on to a plate and placing it in front of her. Eden bit her lip and looked up at him.

'I thought you ate your breakfast on the patio. I don't want to disrupt your routine.'

'Calm down,' he advised, sitting opposite her. 'It's im-material to me where I eat, and if I'm going to be listening to a story I might as well do so in here and not outside where I'd likely be distracted by the birds and the sounds of the morning—not to mention the fact that I'd automatically be squinting down at the sea to discover whether or not Eden Dare was dicing with death in the surf—which incidentally is pretty wild today.'

'I don't take chances,' she said stiffly. 'I don't want you to waste your valuable time coming to save my life.'

'Do I detect a certain note of sarcasm?' he asked with a slight smile, and disconcerted her with his green stare. 'But to get back to the story—you were on the point of telling me about these interests of yours. Such as what, for instance?'

'Well, pottery, I suppose,' she admitted, a little confused by the digression.

'Why pottery?'

She shrugged, her eyes dreamy. 'My father was a potter, and until he died—when I was thirteen—I was always playing about with clay. I loved it. You could just about say I was born with a lump of clay in my hand.'

'And you couldn't follow it up because you had more pressing duties to perform in the way of keeping the money coming in to support yourself and your mother. Is that it?'

'Yes,' she agreed.

He reached for the coffee, and poured it into two mugs he had previously taken from the dresser. They were handmade pottery mugs, a fact which she had already automatically observed—a rich dark brown in colour, with a streaky ivory-coloured glaze that covered the upper two-thirds and the handle. Eden looked up from admiring the one he had handed her and met his eyes. 'These are—good. I like them.'

'My sister's work,' he said. 'It might interest you to know that Lorraine has a studio and a small kiln at the back of the bungalow here. But perhaps you know that already.'

'How would I know?' she asked, and then blushed crimson, remembering how he had caught her that first day, hands cupped around her face, peering in his window. She stared at him belligerently. 'You think I looked in all your windows! I didn't—I——'

'You're jumping to conclusions,' he interrupted dryly. 'I simply thought Amy might have mentioned it, so don't get so worked up.' He stirred two spoonfuls of sugar into his coffee and looked at her consideringly, one green eye screwed up. 'Now let's see what point we've reached in this setting straight process. I think you aimed to demonstrate I'd formed a wrong impression of you at our first meeting, and up to a point I'm willing to concede I had. If you're interested, I thought you were probably a spoiled only child who'd come tootling out from England on a holiday of indefinite length, possibly hoping to ingratiate yourself with your Australian grandfather. Though it was plain you weren't making much of a fist of that.'

'My grandfather and I just—just didn't get on well together.'

He nodded. 'I could see that. And perhaps it's no wonder. Elderly people often don't care for kids who answer back, and you're more than a little too ready with your tongue and your temper, aren't you? It's something that takes a bit of getting used to even when it's directed at someone of my age.'

'I generally—try to control it,' she said uncertainly.

'But not in your dealings with me,' he suggested.

She shrugged. 'Anyhow, my grandfather has a biting tongue too, though of course he blames my fault on the other side of the family. My mother used to flare up too, but she was quick to apologise and very warmhearted, which he isn't. He thinks he's a paragon. At least I'm aware of the fact that I say things I shouldn't have.'

She paused, and he put in dampeningly, 'I still think

87

your grandfather had plenty of room for complaint about your behaviour.'

'But he didn't,' Eden said stubbornly. She drew a deep breath. 'That's the whole thing. You see, what really happened that day——' She stopped. Because at that inconvenient moment, someone rang the doorbell.

Sin grimaced. 'Excuse me.' He rose and left the room, and in her head Eden continued to explain about Berry Addison's conscienceless behaviour and her own helplessness in view of the fact that her grandfather had already made up his mind about her. Once she had persuaded him she was a perfectly normal and trustworthy girl, she would go on to tell him about Amy's change of plans, and to promise him that she would take the utmost care of every scrap of Christie Vaughan's property if only he would go away. Though of course she wouldn't put it like that ...

She was feeling just faintly amused at this thought when the voices of which she had been only partly aware came closer, and the next instant, Sin came into the kitchen accompanied by Don and Bibi Webster.

'Hello!' said Bibi, dropping down into a chair and shooting Eden a not particularly friendly smile. 'I hope we're not interrupting anything. We've been looking for Amy, but the door was locked and we couldn't find a soul, so we came over to Sin's. He says Amy hasn't arrived.'

'No.' Eden swallowed down the remains of her coffee, aware from Bibi's manner and that phrase about 'not interrupting anything' that it must look distinctly odd for her to be here sharing breakfast with Sin Watermount. She was relieved when Sin said calmly, 'I suggest we all transfer to the patio. The kitchen's no place for four people on a hot morning. Coffee for you, Bibi?—Don? And what about Eden? Another cup?'

Eden had time to recover from her embarrassment during the next few minutes, but once they were all settled outside she had to face Bibi again and also to think up an answer to the question, 'When are you expecting Amy?'

'Not today,' she said brightly, because it wasn't really a strategic moment to tell the truth.

'I'll tell you why I ask,' said Bibi, sharp-eyed. 'Don and I are all set for a week's holiday which Dad has granted us after a lot of urging, and as Christie practically promised we'd be able to stay in her bungalow with Amy, we came straight here.'

Eden, listening, was aware of a mixture of feelings. Relief because it looked as though she was no longer going to be on her own, uncertainty because she didn't know whether or not she should accept house guests in a bungalow that was not her own. She felt an almost irresistible urge to look to Sin for advice or for a lead at least, but of course, he expected Amy to be on the scene at almost any minute. So she must make up her own mind, and since Christie had been in favour of a romance between Amy and Don, she was inclined to conclude that Christie would want the Websters to stay in her house. She told Bibi brightly, 'Of course you must stay here then. I'm just sorry Amy isn't here.' A glance at Sin showed her that he was frowning. Oh well, even if he disapproved of her playing the hostess it was nothing to do with him, she told herself determinedly. He could like it or lump it, and if he had any sense, he'd see that here was his opportunity to disappear from the scene.

'Did you say Amy will be here tomorrow?' Bibi demanded, as she stared inscrutably at Eden over her coffee mug.

Eden tried to look unperturbed. 'No, I didn't. As a matter of fact,' she hurried on, 'she probably won't be here for a couple of weeks. She's been invited to stay with some friends down the coast.' Sin had turned in her direction—she could positively feel his eyes boring into her even before she forced herself to meet his gaze and say blatantly, 'I hadn't got around to telling you that, Sin. I—er—I just heard from her.'

He didn't believe a word of that, of course, and she knew with a sinking feeling that all her plans had come to nothing. She hadn't told him the things she had meant to, and now he was looking more than ever as if he wouldn't trust her an inch. Well, he didn't have to, and unless he thought he could contend with three people living next door, and likely to disturb him just a little more than one person, then he would pack his bags and—what was the expression he had used?—tootle off.

All the same, she had an odd sensation of having let herself down in not having got around to explaining that sordid business at Overlooking to him. Now, she would probably never get the chance.

Back at the bungalow a short time later, it was decided that Eden should stay in the bedroom she was presently using, Bibi would occupy Christie's room, and Don would have the third bedroom. Don arranged his belongings speedily and asked if either of the girls wanted to come down to the lagoon with him. Neither of them did, and he drove off on his own while Bibi installed herself and her belongings in Christie's room.

'Come and talk to me,' she told Eden, and Eden watched as she swept the decorative doll off the big double bed and left it slumped against the wall. 'I've grown out of dolls even if Christie hasn't,' she said unconcernedly. 'Now tell me what's happened to Amy.'

'Oh, nothing,' said Eden. 'She's gone to stay with a family, that's all. People I don't know.'

Bibi opened the wardrobe to find it crammed with clothes, pulled open a couple of drawers and found them in use too. She moved around the room opening every cupboard and every drawer as if she had a perfect right to do so, and at last Eden said edgily, 'Would you rather have the room I'm in, Bibi? It's—empty. I can keep my things in a suitcase, I don't have much.'

'Oh, don't fuss,' said Bibi. 'I'll be perfectly happy here, and I like this big room.' She dragged open the lid of a sea-chest at the foot of the bed, a very old-looking and solid piece of cedar. It was full of blankets and bed linen, and she let the lid bang down and set her open suitcase on top of it. 'I guess that belonged to poor old William Vaughan. What were you doing at Sin Watermount's so early in the morning, Eden?' she continued without a pause. 'Do you often share breakfast with him? It all looked mighty suspicious, Sin in nothing but that towelling robe——'

'And me fully dressed,' Eden said sharply, though she had coloured deeply. 'I'd just—just called in to discuss something with him—to tell him about Amy,' she added wildly.

Bibi smiled disbelievingly. 'Everyone falls for Sin,' she commented. She rooted out of her suitcase the smallest bikini Eden had ever seen, and slung it on to the pretty Spanish bedcover. 'Well, now I'm here you're going to find the competition's keen.'

Eden blinked and said coldly, 'I haven't fallen for Sin. Besides, he's Christie Vaughan's property.'

'Oh, piffle,' said Bibi, pulling her cotton shirt over her head. 'He's in the process of wriggling right off her sharp little barbed hook, if you ask me.' She tossed down her skin-coloured bra and put on her bikini top. It was lime green and so tiny that it was almost indecent. Not the sort of thing Eden could ever imagine herself wearing, though lots of girls did. The lower half of it fastened at the sides with rings and narrow loops so that the utmost of bare skin was exposed. Bibi kicked her skirt out of the way and went to stand in front of the big mirror that covered most of one wall while she brushed her coppery hair. She was far from beautiful, her freckled face was unremarkable except for those glowing brown eyes, but in a bikini she was really something to look at. Her figure was perfect, narrow-waisted with a voluptuous bosom and hips, and practically none of its charms hidden by the two tiny green lime green scraps.

Tossing her brush down on the dressing, table she flipped up the lid of a silver box and said, 'Ah!' as she extracted a few snapshots and began examining them. Eden's lips parted in protest, but she had already gathered that there was nothing she could do about Bibi. Bibi would do whatever she wanted to do, regardless of what Eden thought.

'Boy-friends by the dozen,' said Bibi, flipping through the photos. 'And every one of them disappointed. There's Don, and here's—oh, here's one who wasn't disappointed. I'll bet he didn't ask for much.' Looking at the back of the print, she read out flippantly, 'For my baby doll, from her ever grateful William.' Her bright brown eyes went mockingly to Eden. 'Grateful for what, I wonder? She didn't give him any children. It amazes me that they actually possessed a double bed. I wonder what possessed her to have it transported down here? Of course it's nice for the kewpie doll, but that's about all.' She looked at Eden, who was listening with distaste. 'You think I'm talking off the top of my head, don't you? But I'm Don's sister, and I know Don didn't get anything but flirtation and frustration from Christie Vaughan. A bit kinky from a young widow, wouldn't you say?' She flicked the photo in Eden's direction and it fell on the floor. 'William was just a nice old man, and that's what she liked. And then there was all that lovely money . . . Well, I'm going down to the beach, that's what I'm here for.'

She fished in her suitcase again and produced a tan and yellow surf towel and sunglasses. Khu Khan appeared in the doorway, took one blue-eyed look at her, and whisked off again.

'Birrie Beach isn't safe,' Eden warned rather coolly. She was stunned by Bibi's behaviour and by her talk—her head was still reeling. 'Sin—Sin said the surf's wild today.'

'So what?' said Bibi. 'I'll get Sin to come with me—that will make it all the more dangerous, won't it?' She smiled and widened her eyes, then began to trail through the house. 'What's there to drink in the fridge? I'll take a bottle of Coke or something.'

In the sitting room she picked up the portrait of Sin and carried it back to the bedroom where she put it on the bedside table, and Eden felt her resentment and dislike growing.

'Sin works in the mornings,' she said, following Bibi to the kitchen. 'You shouldn't disturb him. He's had a swim already, anyhow.'

Bibi, the fridge door open, stared at her in amazement. 'Are you telling me what to do? If so—by what right? Can't Sin and I work it out between us without your interference? And don't tell me you have first claim.'

'I'm not talking about claims,' Eden interrupted, trying not to lose her temper. 'I just don't think you should bother him, that's all.'

'You *are* virtuous, aren't you?' Bibi said with something like a sneer, and a contemptuous look at Eden's pink dress. 'No one would ever think you'd been caught breakfasting next door. But don't try to jostle me out of the queue. I like Sin a lot and he likes me, as you may have observed on Christmas Day.'

Eden was shaken. It was true enough she supposed that Sin and Bibi had spent a fair bit of time alone on Christmas Day. She said stammeringly, 'But—Christie——'

'Oh, Christie! Christie would never marry a man as red-blooded as Sin.' Bibi took a bottle of Coke from the fridge and slamming the door shut, tucked the bottle under her arm and flipped her fingers. 'Christie's not on the scene. And as far as I'm concerned, she's just a predatory female. She latched on to a rich old man before she'd even begun to earn her living. Nursing was too much like real life. Now with him out of the way and a great fat bank account, she expects every man she meets to fall at her feet. Don did just that, and she dropped him the minute Sin came back here from Bangkok. But she can't have it all her own way. Sin wouldn't have made up excuses for dropping out of the holiday jaunt for nothing.'

'He didn't make up excuses,' said Eden coldly, and reflected that it was odd for her to be defending Sin Watermount in any way at all. But Bibi was such bad taste! 'He has a lot of work to do, and some important research in Canberra. The only reason he hasn't gone yet is he didn't want to leave me on my own here before Amy came, if you want to know.'

Bibi raised her eyebrows. 'Well, you're not on your own now, are you? But we'll soon see whether or not he does a disappearing act ... Well, see you later.' And she tripped off.

Eden found she was trembling a little. She tried to put Bibi and her talk out of her mind, but it was impossible. The whole set-up here had altered in a flash, all her own plans had been knocked skew-whiff. She wished now she had said No to Bibi's and Don's moving in instead of being such an easy mark—though she had a feeling that any opposition she had put up would soon have been overridden. Bibi was not exactly the type to take anything lying down, she was sure of that, and who knew—Sin Watermount might have sided with the Websters, Eden thought pessimistically.

Presently she went into Christie's room, which already

looked a mess with Bibi's clothes scattered all over the place, and took the photograph back to where it belonged in the living room. She paused for a moment to study it thoughtfully, and the look in those very worldly and quite compelling blue-green eyes was hard to fathom. They were somehow very, very masculine, so much harder to read than a woman's eyes.

Right now, she hoped Sin Watermount was putting Bibi well and truly in her place and telling her to—to scoot off.

She moved restlessly to the window and stared through the bush at the sea, where as yet, anyhow, no one appeared to be swimming, though as she couldn't see the beach she didn't know for sure whether Bibi, with or without Sin, had even got that far yet.

The remarks Bibi had made about Christie still rankled. What a cheek, Eden thought, grey eyes narrowed, to come and stay in someone's house—take over their very bedroom —and then run them down! Certainly Bibi was no friend of Christie's. For her part, Eden had no doubts at all about Christie Vaughan's character. Even apart from Amy's opinion of her cousin, there was that photograph of a girl who looked utterly open and charming. She just was *not* a predatory female, luring men on and dropping them.

No, as far as Eden was concerned Christie Vaughan was thoroughly nice, too nice in fact for a man as hard and critical and censorious as Sin Watermount. But that didn't mean that Bibi should feel at liberty to—to grab him. And Eden just wasn't going to put up with it.

'Not for an instant,' she told herself fiercely, feeling a stirring towards action of some kind. 'I'll go down to the beach and break it up.'

She picked up Khu Khan, who had come inside again and was purring round her feet, and hugged him before she let him go again.

CHAPTER SIX

In her bedroom, Eden got determinedly into her swimsuit. And how modest it looked when she remembered that ultra-modern concoction of Bibi's! Well, probably in a few years' time everyone would be swimming naked. Bibi was just one of the people in the vanguard.

She went through the garden and along the bush track, her head filled with the intense and penetrating sound of cicadas singing in the heat, and when at last she reached the beach there was no one there.

So Bibi must be at Sin Watermount's.

They were sitting at the table on the patio having a drink, she discovered five minutes later. Bibi was drinking Coke straight from the bottle. Almost naked in her bikini, she didn't even have a towel draped over her shoulders, and though Eden wasn't a prude, she was aware that the other girl was deliberately displaying her charms. Sin was wearing sunglasses which made it difficult to tell if he was looking at Bibi or not, but he could hardly help it, Eden supposed.

Bibi took the bottle away from her lips and looked up.

'Were you looking for me, Eden? I hope you haven't come to call me home to lunch already.'

'Nothing was further from my mind,' said Eden, forcing a smile. 'Are you coming down to the beach?'

'With you?' Bibi asked derisively. 'I'm quite happy here in the sun, thanks. The surf's not safe today, anyhow, Sin says.'

Eden looked at Sin. 'We must be interrupting your work,' she said pointedly.

'Oh, don't be such a drag, Eden,' said Bibi. 'This is summer. Sin can't work all day long in heat like this. I've never met anyone so keen on organising other people and telling them what to do. Have you, Sin?'

He shrugged lazily. 'I can't say that's a quality I've particularly observed in Eden. However, it might be an idea for you two girls to run along down to the beach and get on with tanning your hides black. I do have some work I must get on with, charming though I find your company.'

Bibi grimaced. 'We'll get out of your hair, then,' she agreed obligingly. 'Suppose we go into town for dinner tonight. Could you, Sin? Or will you be packing up to leave now Don and I are here? Eden seems to think so.' She looked tauntingly as she spoke.

Sin looked at Eden too, and tilted her a crooked smile. 'I'm afraid I'll be around a while yet, Eden . . . okay, girls, leave me in peace for the rest of the day and we'll make a night of it. I presume Don's available to make four.'

'Probably is,' said Bibi after a second, and Eden was certain she hadn't meant her to be included in the plans for dinner. 'He hasn't a regular girl-friend on his hands at the moment.' She sprang up and nipped quickly round the table to hug Sin and kiss him on the lips, telling him, 'You're a sweetie, Sin. I adore you.'

Eden turned away. It was just too provocative of Bibi, particularly dressed—or undressed—as she was, though certainly Sin looked quite unruffled. Maybe he was used to that kind of behaviour. 'Imagine if I did it,' thought Eden ridiculously. But it was totally impossible to imagine. As for tonight, was she going to come along with Don, if he was available, despite Bibi? Quite honestly, she thought she was.

'I'll see you girls about six-thirty or so,' said Sin, and disappeared into his bungalow.

Eden glanced at the Coke bottle Bibi had left on the

table, the glass Sin had been using, at the ashtray full of cigarette butts. If she'd been Bibi, she'd have wanted to tidy that up. In fact, she found she wanted even though she wasn't responsible for it. But Bibi left it all behind her without a single glance, and trailed off towards the beach remarking rather nastily, 'If Don doesn't turn up this afternoon, Eden, Sin and I will go out on our own. No three-somes.'

Eden didn't answer, she simply followed Bibi down the steep narrow path to the sand. There, both girls spread out their towels and lay on their faces, soaking up the hot sun and not talking. Eden brooded darkly on the little scene she had just broken in on. It was like a picture burned on her retina. She could see distinctly Bibi in her minimal lime green triangles, drinking Coke and smiling at Sin—jumping up to kiss him——

'Oh, the cheek of her!' she thought, and she only just managed not to say it aloud. She sat up and looked help-lessly at the prone female body beside her on the white sand. It was so absolutely obvious that Bibi was setting out to have a flirtation with Sin, or more than that, to take him from Christie, whose right to him she didn't concede in any degree. Eden's nerves were jumping and the pulse at her temples beat double-time as she thought about it all. Then it occurred to her quite suddenly that as well as being responsible for Christie's bungalow and its contents and her cat, she was responsible too for the safety of her boy-friend, Sinclair Watermount—if he would persist in stay-ing around. And just why was he staying around, anyhow, now that Eden was no longer on her own? Was it to enjoy being tantalised by that sexy girl from the banana plan-tation?

'Right,' thought Eden, narrowing her grey eyes and star-ing at the dazzling blue-green of the ocean. 'Right! As from now I appoint myself Sinclair Watermount's keeper.

Little though I like him and little though he likes me, I will cling to him like the proverbial leech. Bibi Webster will just not get a chance to hook her little claws into him.' Where Bibi and Sin Watermount were, there would Eden Dare be too. Threesomes, in fact, would be the rule.

She glanced again at Bibi, who was either asleep or simply in a state of mindlessness. 'Some pretty keen competition is on its way up,' Eden told her silently.

The competition, however, didn't extend to providing Bibi with a rival when it came to dress that night. Eden had only a long terrace dress of black and white cotton, which she wore with long beads and red sandals. Well, she certainly wasn't out to knock Sin Watermount's eye out, that would be beyond her capabilities as well as beyond her desires. All she had to do was to be there.

She was relieved when Don came home soon after five. He had a parcel of huge delectable-looking prawns that he had bought at the beach, and Bibi pounced on them with a cry of, 'Yum, yum! Those will go down with a couple of cans of beer from the fridge!'

'I hope you didn't pick up a date for tonight while you were in town,' she told her brother later as she sprawled on the floor in the pretty sitting room, a can of beer in her hand and the platter of prawns, that Eden and Don had peeled, within easy reach. 'If you have, then Eden's in for a lonely evening—she's been counting on you to escort her to dinner in town to make up a foursome with me and Sin.'

What a way to put it! Eden writhed inwardly. Bibi made it sound as if Eden had made her own arrangements. But Don merely smiled affably and gave her a friendly smile. 'Great! I'll be in that,' he said agreeably.

Eden smiled back at him, then got up from her chair. She had been drinking orange juice, and she didn't want to spoil her dinner by eating too many prawns at this hour. 'I'm going to iron my dress,' she said.

'Oh,' said Bibi clearly, 'the skirt and top I'm wearing are on my bed, Eden. You might see if you think they could do with a run over too.'

Eden didn't answer. She had already discovered that Bibi was a great one for letting other people do things while she sat back. She had let Eden get the lunch, she had let Eden wash up and she hadn't even offered to dry the dishes. She had wandered round the house prying into everything, and then she had spread herself out on the sofa with the fan going and read one of Christie's magazines. She had let Eden and Don peel the prawns, and now she was hoping that Eden would iron her evening gear! But Eden wasn't falling for that, and when she had finished with the iron, she switched it off and left it there in case Bibi wanted it.

She had showered and was in her short cotton house-coat, cutting up the meat for Khu Khan's dinner, some time later when Bibi appeared in the kitchen. The cat, that had been brushing against Eden's bare ankles and uttering a few beguiling miaows, immediately bolted from the room. He didn't like Bibi one bit, that was clear, nor did she like him. Though Sin called him 'it', and 'Christie's animal', there was still somehow a vast difference in their attitudes, and it was telling that Khu Khan never disappeared when Sin was in the vicinity.

Bibi exclaimed, 'Oh, that creepy cat with its ghastly human voice!' She pushed at the flowered bowl with her foot. 'Can't you put that outside for him, for goodness' sake? ... How does my skirt look? I really think it should have been ironed.'

'Well, the iron's there,' said Eden, and added perfunctorily, 'but it looks all right.' She glanced at Bibi as she said it, and blinked slightly. Who was going to notice if Bibi's green and bronze citron skirt was crumpled when she wore a top with such a deeply plunging neckline? Certainly not Sin, thought Eden cynically, and he was as obviously the one who mattered. 'Now if you'll go away, Khu Khan will come back and have his supper,' she told Bibi acidly.

Bibi made a rude face. 'Christie's baby. *Wouldn't* Christie love you? She falls all over anyone who dotes on her cat ... You'd better get a move on or Sin will be here. You are coming, I presume?'

'Of course,' said Eden brightly.

They all went in Sin's car and it turned out to be quite a pleasant evening. Sin had booked a table at a restaurant at the far end of the town—the Silver Prawn, where wide windows gave a vista of the sea and the lights strung out along the beach. There was music, but no dance floor, the menu consisted mostly of local seafood, and Sin had ordered a light white wine, Australian and new to Eden.

From about nine-thirty, the diners were free to provide their own entertainment. This was apparently one of the attractions at the Silver Prawn and some of the guests who sang or played the piano or the guitar were very talented, though there were the usual amateurs who forgot their music or missed top notes, and a few clowns as well, who had everyone in fits of laughter with their fooling.

Eden was taken by surprise when the evening was suddenly over without mishap or unpleasantness of any kind. She had decided that she liked Don, who, in contrast to his sister, didn't have much to say for himself at all, but was thoughtful of her comfort. She had forgotten for some time to keep an eye on Bibi, but there hadn't really been much opportunity for outrageously flirtatious behaviour, and when Sin drove them home there were not even any goodnight kisses. It had all, in fact, been very painless indeed.

Next morning, without saying a word, Bibi disappeared straight after breakfast. She hadn't made her bed, and the dishes weren't done—that was left to Eden, for Don was

101

fixing up his fishing gear outside. Eden asked him, 'Where's Bibi?' and he told her carelessly, 'Gone for a swim, I expect.'

For a swim or to the bungalow next door? Eden wondered. She sighed when she thought of tailing Bibi, but she supposed she must do it. For Christie's sake. She left the dishes, changed into her swimsuit, and snatching up a book and her towel, hastened through the garden, checking the letter box as she went. This time Bibi was on the beach, alone. Her bikini was sea-blue, and just as revealing as the other one.

She greeted Eden quite pleasantly from where she was lying on the sand. 'Hello! Are you coming into the surf? I consulted the oracle and we're safe today—no nasty rips to carry us out to sea.' She got up and Eden saw she had a rubber surf-board with her, and when presently they went into the water together, Bibi was soon paddling out beyond the breakers, leaving Eden behind on her own.

When Don appeared later to fish off the rocks, Bibi was still floating about on her own, and Eden left the water and went to watch Don, which turned out to be exciting enough, as he was in luck and caught several fish.

Eden cooked the fish for lunch, putting some aside for Khu Khan's dinner. If she had hoped Bibi would do the breakfast dishes while she was preparing the lunch, it was in vain. Bibi showered, then washed her hair and preened herself in Christie's bedroom till lunch was on the table. At the end of the meal, Don disappeared on pursuits of his own and Bibi and Eden sat on and on over their coffee. Eden was waiting to see if Bibi would make the first move to begin the clearing up, but it was pretty obvious that she wouldn't.

When Sin called from the open front door, 'Is anyone at home?' Bibi was immediately on her feet.

'Come on in, Sin—there's still some coffee,' she greeted

102

him, and dashed to the kitchen as though she were a regular little homemaker.

Sin sat down at the table opposite Eden, and for want of something better to say, she remarked, 'I enjoyed last night very much. I don't think I really thanked you for the evening.'

'I hope you gave at least half your thanks to Don,' he said a little dryly. 'We shared the bill, you know.'

Plainly he was pointing out that she hadn't been his guest, and she blushed crimson, and saw his eyes go to her salty, still tangled hair, and the cotton dress she had pulled on.

Bibi appeared triumphantly with the heated-up coffee and an extra cup. She brushed deliberately against Sin as she leaned across his shoulder, her hair gleaming, and freshly scented with Eden's shampoo. Eden felt a mess. She was also aware that the house looked a mess, and she was sure Sin had noted that too.

'Ready for that drive up the coast, Bibi?' Sin asked presently, and Bibi nodded, shooting a triumphant glance in Eden's direction. 'I'll give you a quarter of an hour to get the cleaning-up done.' He took cigarettes from the pocket of his pale beige shirt and rose from the table. 'Okay?'

'I'm practically ready now,' Bibi said airily. 'It's Eden's day to do the work.' Her brown eyes dared to contradict her, for of course they had made no arrangements about taking turns at all. But before Eden could think of a thing to say, Bibi continued, 'You should have played the housewife this morning, Eden, instead of rushing down to the beach as if you were scared you might miss out on something.' Her eyes gleamed maliciously as she whisked herself off to Christie's bedroom to perfect herself for Sin.

Eden knew she had been defeated this time. She could hardly grab her things and say, 'I'm coming too'. Bibi might be able to do it, but not Eden Dare, and she felt her pulses pounding as she fumed inwardly. As a leech she was not being particularly successful, and she looked angrily at Sin, who was lighting a cigarette.

He met her eyes as he flicked off his lighter, and asked, 'You don't smoke, do you?'

'No, thank you,' she said shortly.

'What's troubling you? Why the concentrated disapproval?'

Had it been so plain? She was tempted to answer, 'I don't approve of your gadding about with Bibi when Christie's away', but what was the point? He would probably tell her to mind her own business. She said tartly, 'You're imagining it,' and turned away to start stacking the dishes.

She didn't watch them drive away. Bibi hadn't said whether or not she'd be back for dinner, and Eden almost wished she wouldn't. But whether she was or not, there was essential shopping to do. The bread and milk were disappearing fast and so were the fruit and fresh vegetables. It simply didn't seem to occur to Bibi or Don to replenish the stock. Eden would have to do that. All the same, she wasn't prepared to use up all her savings feeding three, so with some regret she took five dollars from the Chinese vase. There was nothing dishonest about it, Christie had said to use it, but she had been so determined to be independent and to leave that money intact.

As she cycled in to town through the hot afternoon, she couldn't keep her mind from those two who had gone off in Sin's car up the coast, with Bibi looking exciting in a white cotton sun-dress that showed off her figure. Eden knew by now that no one could consider Bibi plain. That figure! And those glowing eyes! The phrase 'come-to-bed-eyes' flitted into Eden's mind, it was so terribly apt. It certainly looked as though she were letting Christie down today. She just didn't see how she was going to hold the fort even a week if Sin was prepared to take time off from his work to drive Bibi about the countryside.

She wondered where Don was, and discovered as she rode slowly along by the shores of the lagoon that he was there, paddling around in a boat which he must have hired, and all on his own. She didn't hurry over her shopping, because she felt decidedly lonely. In a way she wished she had never come to the coast. She had imagined it would be great with Amy here, the two of them swimming together and meeting people. As it was, she had met no one but Sin Watermount, and now more trouble—the Websters. But she was determined that what had happened this afternoon was not going to happen again.

Bibi was intent on mischief and so, for all she knew, was Sin—Christie's dreamboat, thought Eden as she pedalled furiously home lateish in the afternoon. Well, they were not going to get away with it. 'If I have to monopolise him myself,' thought Eden, 'he's going to be all in one piece when Christie comes back.'

Don came home soon after she did, and she made a pot of tea and finished putting her shopping away. She heard Sin's car drive past, but Bibi didn't appear, so they must be having a cosy little get-together at his bungalow. If it had been Eden, she'd have been put out at the gate and sent home. Sin wasn't the sort of man who would be pushed into anything that didn't suit him ...

She told Don, 'I'm going to look for Khu.' She knew very well that the cat was stretched out in the shade on the cool sandstone slab by the back door, but that was a mere detail. She went straight through the bush to Sin's garden and began to call the cat's name. When she reached the corner of the house it was all she could manage not to turn and flee as she saw Bibi and Sin standing under the jasmine vine. Sin's hands were linked behind her waist and her face was turned up to his as if they had been kissing.

Which, to judge by the satisfied expression on Bibi's face as she turned towards Eden, they certainly had been doing.

Eden gritted her teeth. It was not her thing at all to be breaking in on love scenes this way, but she stood her ground and said distinctly, despite hot cheeks, 'Oh, excuse me—I'm looking for Christie's animal.'

Bibi plainly didn't believe her, but Sin looked amused and not in the least embarrassed, and his green eyes glinted as he suggested, 'You should try whistling, Eden. That way Bibi and I might have been warned, and as well, the *animal* might have materialised.'

'I'm not an expert at whistling,' she improvised swiftly. 'But I *was* calling him. You'd have heard me if you hadn't been so busy,' she finished sarcastically.

Sin let Bibi go and came across the flagging, and he was —oh, he was swaggering, she thought in exasperation, in such an arrogant male way, as though it were just part of the day's work to go around kissing anyone he pleased while his fiancée was out of the way! Eden felt so thoroughly incensed that she found she was glaring at him savagely.

'What's the matter?' he asked softly as he came closer to her. 'You look ready to kill someone. Has Christie's animal done some damage at the bungalow?'

'No,' she snapped. 'Khu Khan hasn't done any damage— *he* knows how to behave himself!'

A spark of anger showed in his green eyes, but he merely lifted his brows fractionally. He didn't offer to whistle for Khu Khan, which showed that he didn't believe her story, and Bibi said decidedly, 'That stupid cat's not here, Eden. Sin and I were just about to go in and get a drink. Why don't you go home and get the tea ready?'

Eden simply couldn't swallow down her anger. That contemptuous tone! In the name of heaven, who did Bibi think Eden was that she could order her about? Grey eyes flashing, she snapped back, 'Why don't *you*?' Bibi had come to stand at Sin's shoulder and put one arm possessively around his waist, her hand resting on his hip. 'Don's the one with the big appetite—and he's your brother, not mine.'

Bibi smiled and remained infuriatingly unperturbed. 'It's still your day for the house,' she insisted. 'And I had the idea you were keen on impressing Don with your various talents—that's how it's looked so far, anyhow.'

Eden felt herself go white with anger. Part of her wanted to be done with it all, to let Bibi do what she liked. But another part of her refused to be routed, and she felt herself hating Bibi Webster with a disconcerting intensity —'Coming here and spoiling everything,' she thought, then amended that mentally to 'complicating everything'. She didn't know quite what would have happened next if Sin hadn't said, as Bibi shrugged and headed for the open door of the house,

'Calm down now, Eden.' He was watching her narrowly, an odd expression that was half amusement, half something else, in his blue-green eyes. 'Come in and have a drink, anyhow, and then you two girls can go back and prepare dinner together. Amicably, it's to be hoped.'

Head high, and feeling the smart of unexpected tears in her eyes, Eden said tensely, 'Thank you.' Hating it, *hating* to have to go in and make a threesome, but simply refusing to give in despite the awkwardness. Sin put his hand lightly on her shoulder and she shook it off. 'Don't touch me!' She thought wildly, 'What on earth must he think?' Her feeble excuse about Khu Khan hadn't fooled anyone, and she wondered exactly *why* he thought she had come traipsing down here. She knew well enough how Bibi would interpret it—that Eden wanted Sin for herself. Well, she was quite wrong, and surely Sin Watermount must know that wasn't so! *He* knew that Eden Dare couldn't stand him at any price!

He had dropped his hand from her shoulder, and he said musingly, 'By the way, I never discovered what all that straightening out business was about the other day. We must take that conversation up again some time.'

'Oh, forget it. It doesn't matter,' Eden got out. She moved ahead of him into the house where Bibi was making herself very much at home. She had opened up the cocktail cabinet as if it were her own, and was setting glasses on a tray.

'What will you have, Eden?' she asked with a malicious smile. 'I guess you could do with a stiff whisky.'

'I'll fix the drinks,' Sin said, taking over masterfully. Bibi stayed to hang over his shoulder, while Eden, ridiculously and humiliatingly close to tears, sat down in one of the soft black leather chairs, clenching her fists and wondering wretchedly, 'Is it worth it?' Christie would probably be well rid of him.

She hoped her mixed emotions weren't showing as she took the glass Sin presently handed her, with a murmured 'Thanks.'

'That will pep you up,' he said with a smile, and somehow she managed to smile back at him. His eyes lingered thoughtfully on her face. She supposed she hadn't smiled at him often, and nor had he smiled at her, and this was an odd time for it to be happening. His teeth showed white against his tan, and his eyes were intent on hers, and she suddenly lowered her lashes, half defensive, half puzzled.

He allowed them only one drink and then with a decision that was not to be argued with, he told them, 'Time for the parting of the ways. You girls have a hungry man to feed.'

They walked home in silence, and when they went into the house it was to discover that Don had gone out, leaving a note to the effect that he would be late for dinner. Khu Khan came miaowing out to the kitchen. Tonight he ignored Bibi, and concentrated all his attention on Eden, who proceded to prepare his fish for him.

Bibi, leaning against the counter, her claws well and truly out now they were alone, said quarrelsomely, 'You had a hide, chasing me down there. Why didn't you disappear when you saw that Sin and I wanted to be alone? You're just as jealous as can be——'

Eden looked up and said coldly, 'Make up your mind, Bibi. Who am I supposed to want? Don? Or Sinclair Watermount?'

'Both, is my guess,' said Bibi, her brown eyes spiteful. She looked disparagingly at the cat, who was now eating his fish dinner.

'What utter drivel!' exclaimed Eden. 'I like Don, but you know very well I don't run after him. And Sin is Christie Vaughan's property, a fact which I respect, though you obviously don't.'

Bibi smiled aggravatingly. 'It takes two to tango, Eden! Sin can say no if he wants to, and as far as I'm concerned he's not anyone's property till he's well and truly married. Sin and I like each other—but you can forget him.'

'I don't need to,' snapped Eden, and added to her own surprise, 'I happen to have a boy-friend of my own, anyhow.'

'Lucky you,' said Bibi maddeningly. Then—'What's for dinner?'

'Whatever you like to get,' said Eden through her teeth. 'Look in the fridge. I'm not hungry.'

Khu Khan had finished his fish and disappeared, and Eden turned her back on Bibi and did likewise. She walked straight out the front door and through the garden. She simply couldn't stay alone in the house with Bibi a moment longer. Oh, how peaceful it had been before the Websters came, despite her feud with Sin, she thought desolately. She felt again that she hated Bibi, and the vehemence of her emotions shocked her. There was really nothing wrong with Bibi, except that she had this crush on Sin and was determined to get a response from him. She was getting it, too, Eden thought, plunging through the bush.

It was a darkish night, the sky was covered with scudding clouds and the air was warm and heavy with flower perfumes and the tangy scent of eucalyptus. There were lights in Sin's bungalow, and an outside light made shadows amongst the banksias and tea trees as she flitted through them and reached the path to the beach. She made her way down cautiously, finding the concentration good for her nerves and helpful towards forgetting Bibi and that undignified squabble in the kitchen. The sea was still noisy and the roar the breakers made as they came foaming in over the sand was somehow therapeutic.

Eden kicked off her sandals and wandered down to the hard wet sand, feeling it cool beneath her bare feet. Far out on the horizon she could see the lonely lights of a ship that moved slowly south, to disappear from her view now and again as some extra large wave came thundering in to crash gaspingly into splinters of foam.

'Every ninth wave?' Eden wondered. Eyes straining through the darkness, she wandered along in the shallow water counting. She had reached no conclusion when suddenly she was almost up to her waist in swirling dark water. She gasped as she felt the outward drag and braced her legs to resist it. A little crazily under the circumstances, she remembered something Sin Watermount had once said—that the sea is as capricious and as dangerous as love. 'Before you know what's happening it can carry you somewhere you don't want to be.'

Well, this time she had won, she reflected, when the water had receded, and on the verge of nervous laughter, she turned and fled across the sand to safety, her cotton trousers clinging to her legs.

She was brought up with a shock as she collided with a dark form that suddenly loomed up in front of her. For an instant her body was pressed against another, and then she felt the warmth of strong hands on her upper arms as she stepped back, gasping a little. She knew who it was, and her heart beat wildly.

'Eden Dare,' said Sin Watermount, his voice slightly muffled by the roar of the waves, 'aren't you reckless to be playing games with the sea in the dark? Or are you intent on drowning yourself?'

The sea—love—— She felt oddly confused.

'I'm—I'm not trying to drown myself,' she said huskily, a little too conscious of those fingers that gripped her arms so firmly. 'It was—just one wave bigger than the rest——'

'One wave is all that's needed,' he said sharply, and his hands tightened briefly before he released her. 'I'd never have seen you if you'd been carried out in the dark, though as a matter of fact I was thinking about you as I walked along the beach. Why aren't you safe at home taking your turn at cooking the dinner?'

'I wasn't hungry. And Bibi and I don't take turns—we haven't made any arrangements so far.' It was all very well protecting Christie, she thought, but Bibi could look after herself. She shivered despite the warmth of the night as she and Sin began to move across the sand towards the upward path. Not looking at him, she asked compulsively, '*Why* were you thinking about me?'

'Why?' She felt rather than saw him shrug. 'I don't know —except that it does seem to have become rather a habit with me lately.'

'Because I'm a—disruptive element in your life?' she asked nervily after a second.

'That would be one way of putting it,' he agreed dryly.

'Then I'm sorry. But you don't have to stay here. Even if the Websters hadn't come, I'm quite—quite trustworthy.'

They had reached the start of the path but neither of them began to climb. Eden's sandals were there where she had left them, and she stooped to pick them up, then stood looking at him through the darkness, deeply aware of him looking back at her. Once one's eyes had become accustomed to the night, it was remarkable how much one could see. She could see the planes of his face, the hard determined line of his jaw, even the lighter streaks in the thick darkness of his hair. But she felt rather than saw the intensity of his gaze.

'I've been puzzling over your trustworthiness,' he said, his voice thoughtful, 'because you didn't cut a very impressive figure at our first encounter. You were really in trouble, weren't you, and no wonder—playing around with the truth, evasive when you should have been honest. And while I can't pretend I admired your boy-friend, at least he had the sense to know when the game was up.'

'That was what I wanted to straighten out,' she said at once. 'You're quite wrong about Berry and me. I—I wasn't playing around with the truth. I didn't know what had happened to that painting—it was Berry who lied when he said I'd agreed to his taking it. My grandfather accepted his word because he just doesn't want to believe good of me. He never forgave my mother for running away and marrying a man of whom he didn't approve.' She stopped, but the man who stood so close to her in the darkness said nothing, and presently she said resentfully, 'You still don't believe me, do you?'

He said from above her, his voice cool, tolerant, 'I think you should take more care in choosing your friends.'

'One doesn't choose friends,' she retorted rashly. 'One just—makes them. I don't expect people to be perfect—I don't walk round and round checking for faults. Anyhow, if it's of any interest to you, Berry and I are through, and I've left Overlooking and I'm never going back.' She pulled on her sandals and started to climb up the path, groping her way in the dark. Sin hadn't apologised for misjudging her, he hadn't even said he believed her, and in spite of herself, she felt deeply wounded. He was obviously the sort of man you couldn't explain anything to, she thought bitterly. If he didn't like you then he didn't like you. Now if she were Bibi Webster, she could tell him anything at all and he'd accept it.

She was nearing the top of the climb and he was close behind her when she said breathlessly, 'I don't know why I bother talking to you. You don't like me and—and I couldn't care less.'

She gasped as he suddenly seized her round the waist, and she all but overbalanced on the rough path. Then he had swung her round to face him in the dark shelter of a twisted banksia tree.

'I never knew you wanted me to like you, Eden Dare.' He had bent his head and she could feel the movement of his breath as he spoke. 'Ever since you came here, you seem to have been quite determined I shouldn't do that. But as a matter of fact, I find you damnably attractive—and not merely on account of the rather unusual brand of prettiness you sport. Only let me tell you it's all against my better judgement, because you're a proper little nitwit, and every time you open your mouth you ask for trouble ... No, you're not at all the sort of girl who usually appeals to me.'

Eden's breath came fast and she struggled against some chaotic emotion that she didn't even try to analyse. She heard herself say indistinctly, 'I'm not a nitwit—and—and I'm not in the least interested in your finding me attractive, so don't imagine you can flatter me by your patronising remarks. And now please let me go. I can't stand around all night in wet clothes.'

His hands moved slightly on her waist but he didn't let her go. 'Your clothes are all but dry,' he said laconically. His face was close to hers, and she had a sudden vision of him kissing Bibi this evening on the patio. It was probably that that made her say nervily, 'I—I don't want to be kissed, thank you, Mr Watermount.'

'Then you shouldn't talk about kissing,' he said with a low laugh. 'Now you've given me the idea, I think it's a decidedly agreeable one.'

'Not to me,' she got out. Her heart was thudding and the blood was rising in her cheeks. She simply hadn't bargained on this sort of thing from Sin Watermount, and if he didn't let her go in a second she was going to fight herself free. But she let it go a second too long.

'No fighting?' he said softly, his face hovering above hers.

So she had to play it with dignity. 'I'm not the scratching and biting type,' she said with the merest tremor in her voice. 'I expect people to be—reasonable. You're—you're making a nuisance of yourself.'

She saw his eyebrows rise. 'You can't be serious! A kiss is nothing.'

'I daresay. But I happen to be particular who I kiss and who kisses me. I know you haven't a great opinion of my character, but it's against my principles to poach on someone else's preserves.'

'Kisses and principles and preserves,' he murmured. 'What a mixture to administer at a moment like this!' Regardless of her wishes, his lips were about to claim hers when he raised his head and said laconically, 'We're about to be discovered in incriminating circumstances. Someone is looking for one—or both—of us.'

He let her go, and through the pounding of her heart Eden heard another sound—soft footsteps through the trees. She moved away from him and stumbled through the bush.

It was Bibi, of course, and in the light from Sin's garden lamp, Eden saw the fury on her face as she and Sin appeared. Bibi quickly composed her features, however, and actually managed a bright smile as she asked, her voice high-pitched and incredulous, 'Have you been fishing Eden out of the sea, for goodness' sake, Sin?'

'I was too late to do that. We met up as I was returning from a solitary walk intended to give me an appetite for dinner. Eden will no doubt tell you how she came to be wading in the sea fully clad. I'll hand her over to your tender care.'

'It's long past dinner time,' Bibi said snappily, her attention returning to Eden. 'I've been looking for you all over the place. I don't know what that boy-friend you're always raving about would think if he knew you were following Sin down to the beach in the dark.'

'Eden's safe enough with me,' Sin said casually, though his eyes were sharp.

'Not all that safe,' thought Eden cynically, whose ears were tingling from Bibi's calculated remark about her boyfriend. When it came to imagination Bibi certainly deserved a prize, and now Eden turned away from both of them. 'I'm going home to change. Goodnight, Sin.'

'Goodnight.' It sounded abrupt and she didn't know whether he and Bibi had anything more to say to each other as she hurried away.

Bibi caught her up before she reached the door and said nastily, 'Your clothes aren't all wet—though they obviously have been. How long have you been hanging about in the dark with Sin, I'd like to know?'

'Would you? Well, actually I have no idea,' said Eden brightly. 'I don't have a watch.' She marched ahead and once in her room shut the door firmly before stripping off her clothes that were sticky with salt. She decided to postpone her shower till after dinner, seeing that the meal must be ready. Freshly dressed, she turned to the mirror to brush out her hair, and her grey eyes, golden-flecked near the pupils, looked back at her warily. 'Even apart from your unusual brand of prettiness,' she heard Sin's voice saying, 'I find you damnably attractive.'

She bit her lip. Oh God, what was she thinking about? His mouth had touched hers briefly and then Bibi had been there ... All this time while Christie thought he was locked up in some library poring over books, he was in fact making love to other women. 'I wouldn't trust him an inch,' thought Eden, tossing down her brush and turning away from her reflection.

In the living room, she found dinner not ready after all, and the two Websters were sitting back watching a television programme. She stood surveying them exasperatedly till Bibi raised her head and said casually, 'Oh, you're there, Eden. I haven't started cooking the fish yet. You made such a good job of it last time that Don and I decided to leave it to you again. Okay?' She smiled, but not with her eyes.

'Okay,' Eden said. What else was there to say? She knew that Bibi must be wondering exactly what had happened between herself and Sin. Well, nothing had happened—nothing at all, she thought as she went into the kitchen.

Yet while she assured herself quite firmly of this, somewhere in the dark recesses of her mind she knew it was not altogether true, and that if she allowed herself to go on thinking about it, she just might uncover something that she would find unacceptable ...

CHAPTER SEVEN

SIN stayed in his bungalow working all next day. That at least was the information Bibi brought back to the house just as Eden was reluctantly preparing to follow her down to the beach. She was dreading it today, and wondering if it was all worthwhile. Why not leave Sin and Bibi to their own devices? All this squabbling and chasing each other—because Bibi was doing it too—was so undignified. Eden's thoughts on the matter were confused and her head was aching, so it really was a relief when Bibi brought the news, even though she did end spitefully, 'So you can resign yourself to wasting your sweetness on the desert air if you do go down to the beach. Sin's busy and he's going to stay that way till dinner tonight. I've invited him here for that.'

Before Eden could make up her mind what to do, whether to continue as though what she did had nothing to do with Sin or Bibi, or whether to tidy up the bungalow which seemed to have got into quite a state of untidiness in the last couple of days, Don appeared with the suggestion that they should all motor up the coast to a beach where, from his past experience, the fishing was particularly good.

Eden went, because she couldn't face the idea of being here alone even though Sin *was* working, and because Bibi urged her to come, ostensibly because, as she said, 'You can have a better time when there are two—it's easier to pick up with a crowd. Don will be fishing all day if I know him.'

Don did fish most of the day, and it was as Bibi had said. The girls hadn't long installed themselves to sunbathe on the sand when two presentable males took up a position

117

close by, and in a few minutes they were exchanging chit-chat. Bibi—obviously to Eden—picked out which one was to be her property, and the rest of the day was passed swimming, flirting, and drinking beer from cans. They lunched at a beach restaurant where they were joined by another group and the afternoon was noisy and convivial, though for her part Eden found herself not terribly entertained, and actually went to sleep in the shade of some paperbarks.

When she woke Don was there with a nice haul of fish, the party was breaking up, and Bibi wanted to discuss dinner plans.

'D'you think we should buy some prawns and make a curry? We need more than just fish with Sin coming. Don can buy a couple of bottles of wine at the pub across the road. What do you think, Eden?'

Eden smiled wryly to herself. Quite plainly she was to be the cook once more, she thought, even though the dinner party was Bibi's.

'All right,' she said agreeably. 'We'll buy some prawns, but serve them as a cocktail, I think. We can cook the fish in white wine for a change—I'll show you how.'

'I'd love to learn,' said Bibi enthusiastically. Today she was so affable that it was pleasantly restful, and Eden thought that but for Sin, she and Bibi would have managed to get along together quite well. Sin was the whole trouble—as he always had been.

They packed up their things and crossed the road to the shops, where Eden bought—and paid for—the prawns and Don bought white wine from the bottle department of the hotel, and then they got into the car and made for home.

The telephone rang ten minutes after they arrived. Bibi had gone to take a shower and Don was outside cleaning the fish, so it was Eden who answered it.

'Eden? Sin Watermount here.' A curious little shock

118

went through her system at the sound of his voice. Somehow she had thought—and hoped—that it would be Amy on the phone. 'I heard the car and thought I'd check what time I'm expected.'

She answered flusteredly, 'Bibi's still in the shower and I haven't had mine yet. But—but I suppose you can come any time you like.'

'Right. I'll try to give you time to make yourself pretty.'

'Oh, I shan't be going to any trouble on *your* account,' she said promptly—and unnecessarily, she reflected after she had hung up. She stood for a second wondering if she wished he weren't coming, but in some tense uneasy way she knew she was looking forward to seeing him again, as though she expected evidence that something had changed since his untypical behaviour of last night. Everything, she reflected, as she moved slowly away, had moved into a different focus since the Websters had come . . .

Sin arrived while she was still dressing after her shower. She knew that Bibi was floating around in a long skirt, but perversely she decided to play it down, and got into white pants and a tiny-sleeved top in her favourite violet colour. She emerged from her room apprehensive as to what effect Sin's green stare was going to have on her. The lights weren't on in the living room, the others were sitting sharing a drink in the half-dark, and Sin's eyes were no more than dark shadows as she approached the door and stood ghost-like in her pale colours, unnoticed for a moment.

Earlier on she had opened the wide windows, and outside the day was fading like a flower over the melting warmth of the indigo ocean. The scent of the bush came into the room on a cool breeze, and yellow diamond lights were beginning to spin out along the shore of the distant bay. Eden felt her nerves tingle as her senses stirred to the mood of the evening—a mood that was intensified by the soft music from Christie's record player.

119

She stood listening, half dreaming, and was startled when Sin, rising from his chair, a glass in his hand, moved to greet her with a soft, 'Hello there! Did you have a good day?'

Her eyes met his and she saw—or thought she saw—the flicker of green, and she heard the nervous tattoo of her heart and felt the leap of her nerves. It was a reaction so different from her usual one that she was deeply disturbed. It was a follow-up to last night, of course, but that episode was closed—finished. She wanted to forget Sin's meaningless remark that he found her 'damnably attractive', yet—yet she couldn't. It buzzed and hovered like a stupid insistent bee at the back of her mind.

Now as she met his eyes she felt a terrible confusion. Last night was suddenly as close as Sin himself, and her eyes went to his mouth and her heart thudded so loudly that she wondered for a crazy moment if he could actually hear it—if he knew without even touching her that her pulse was racing. There was a faint smile on his lips as though he were amused by her, and instantly she was annoyed. She had better stop standing here like a stunned mullet, as Amy would have put it, all ready to reach melting point. The truth was, she told herself sternly, that Eden Dare felt exactly the same about Sin Watermount as she had always felt. She didn't like him. They just didn't click.

She turned away, not knowing whether she had answered his question or not, and moved to the table where someone had set out drinks. Her hand was shaking as she poured something into a glass.

'I didn't know you were a whisky drinker, Eden,' Sin said mockingly. She had sipped her drink and caught her breath at the fiery taste, and she felt an absolute fool.

She said unsteadily, 'I didn't know we had whisky. I thought—I thought we had only sherry.'

'You did,' he agreed, and he sounded almost comforting. 'I brought my own whisky bottle.' Masterfully, he took her glass from her and poured sherry into a tiny stemmed goblet, and as she took it from him Bibi switched on a reading light.

'You'd better swallow that down quickly,' she told Eden. 'You've been ages getting dressed. We don't want to have dinner too late.'

Eden looked at her quizzically. She was beginning to suspect that Bibi either couldn't cook, or was just bone lazy. She tossed up between saying, 'No, we don't, do we?' and relaxing unconcerned into a chair, or going resignedly kitchenwards. Before she had quite decided, Sin said sardonically, 'Your turn again tonight, Eden? What's it to be?'

She didn't look at him and it was Bibi who answered.

'Fish in white wine. Eden has this beaut recipe she wants to try out.'

And Bibi had said she'd love to learn it. But pretty obviously she wasn't going to learn tonight.

'What about the prawn cocktail, Bibi?' Eden asked innocently, but a little maliciously.

'Oh, I don't have a clue how to manufacture that. It was your idea, anyhow,' Bibi said airily. 'Just at this moment I don't think I could move an inch, I'm so comfortable. You're already up.'

Eden didn't bother protesting. The funny thing was that she hadn't been in the kitchen five minutes when Sin was there too, and in the bright light she had switched on did those too discerning eyes of his linger on her, or was she imagining it? 'I'd better forget the attractive bit,' she thought, 'and remember he called me a nitwit.' That had a decidedly calming effect on her nerves, and she told him briskly, 'You don't need to keep an eye on me. I'm in the

121

kitchen every day and everything still works—even the pop-up toaster. I can even cook, you know—I don't need any help.'

'I didn't come to help. I came to watch—and by that I don't mean what you probably think I mean.'

Now how did she take that? Quite simply, Eden didn't know, and she felt helplessly naïve. She flushed and turned away to the refrigerator. 'I don't like to be watched.'

'By anyone?' He sounded amused. 'Or by me in particular?'

'By—by anyone,' she said after a second.

'You're learning diplomacy,' he congratulated her. 'That tongue of yours usually gets away from you.'

'I told you before, I do try to curb it. It's not something so new, it's due entirely to your gentle influence.'

He laughed in a way that made her nerves tingle, and she decided she would have to ignore him. He had taken a stool on the other side of the kitchen counter, and he sat there with his whisky while Eden prepared the prawn cocktails in little glasses that she had put in the refrigerator to chill earlier. When they were finished, and looking pretty against pale lettuce leaves with their pink dressing gleaming, she put them carefully back in the fridge to keep cool, and turned her attention to the fish, which she had decided to serve with a fairly simple salad, seeing that Bibi hadn't made any suggestions as to accompaniments. Bibi didn't bother coming to help, but she had shifted to another chair from which, Eden noted with wry amusement, she could keep an eye on the two in the kitchen area. Eden laced the fish with herbs, added some thinly sliced onions and drenched it in wine before putting it in the oven to simmer gently. Then she prepared a salad of lettuce and cucumber and tiny radishes, and mixed a simple dressing of oil and vinegar with a dash of tarragon to add at the last minute.

Still taking no notice of Sin, she moved into the dining

area to set the table, and he said lazily, 'You're a model of efficiency tonight, aren't you, Eden Dare? I'll admit I'm surprised.'

She flicked him a glance. 'Are you? That's because you think I'm a nitwit.'

As she put out the place mats and the silver he was still watching her, and she had an impulse to be slapdash, to show him that she wasn't out to impress him, that even if he hadn't been here, dinner would have been exactly the same. Which of course it wouldn't have been. Mainly, of course, she wished he would stop lounging around here and go away.

And at that point in her thoughts he did what she thought she wanted. He strolled back into the other part of the room and she breathed a sigh of relief, and listened as Bibi asked how he was progressing with his book and what it was about.

'It's a mixture of fact and rather wild adventure,' he said with faint amusement. 'The result being, I suppose, a particularly masculine type of fiction.'

To her intense annoyance it was all she heard as Don materialised to ask somewhat belatedly if there were anything he could do.

'I don't think so, except see to the wine.'

'Shall I——' he began without waiting to hear what he was about to ask as she broke in impatiently. 'Oh, don't ask me what you should do, Don. Ask Bibi. It's her dinner party, isn't it?'

Don stared at her in surprise. 'I didn't think it was a dinner party—though you're making a lot of fussy preparations by the look of things, aren't you?'

'If you call making prawn cocktails and cooking some fish and mixing a salad a lot of fussy preparations, then yes, I am,' she said tartly. 'I'm beginning to think we'd all be eating raw fish and prawns out of a paper bag if I didn't do something about it.'

Don stared at her harder, obviously taken aback. 'Oh well, Bibi can't cook,' he said with an uneasy smile. 'And I'm not much of a hand at it except on a bush picnic. I'm sorry, I suppose we're imposing on you.'

Eden felt instantly ashamed and her annoyance vanished. 'Oh, don't apologise, Don. I like cooking really.'

Slightly mollified, he moved off to deal with the wine and Eden heard Sin saying thoughtfully, 'There comes a time when you feel sated with what you've been doing, and in need of a new direction. Not new excitements, but something relevant to the future you envisage for yourself. If you're used to putting situations into words, as I am, then you probably set out to write a book.' He paused and across the distance that separated them Eden caught his eye, and realised he knew she was listening. 'If I turn out something reasonably successful, I'll stay with it, lead a more stable life—make the odd foray to any place that interests, of course; I don't intend to become a recluse.'

'You could never be that,' Bibi said on a laugh. 'No woman would ever allow it.' She glanced up as Eden came across the room. 'There you are, Sin—even Eden's coming to grab her share of your company.'

He got to his feet lazily. 'I rather think Eden's come to summon us to the table to eat the delectable meal she's been preparing. Right, Eden?'

Bibi widened her brown eyes in feigned surprise. 'Dinner already! Oh dear—and I didn't come and do my bit. I hope you've coped, Eden. Is it really to be as delectable as Sin expects?'

Eden couldn't bring herself to make a suitably light-hearted answer. Bibi was infuriating, and as from this moment she could have it all on her own—allot the places, add the finishing touches, play the gracious hostess. But Bibi didn't do any of these things. She was perfectly satisfied to leave it all to Eden. She sat down at the table and didn't give tuppence where anyone else sat, and she ate her prawn cocktail and the delicately flavoured fish without even thinking of expressing approval. However, Eden earned plenty of praise from the menfolk, especially from Don, who was possibly suffering feelings of guilt about imposing on her. Though she felt slightly appeased, her irritation with Bibi was still simmering.

After dinner Sin invited them all to his bungalow for a glass of vintage port, and there they sat outside on the patio, sipping their port and listening to music on cassette tapes. It wasn't long before Don excused himself and went home, and the other three sat on. Don was nice, Eden thought. Very quiet and sort of—young. Both Amy and Bibi had more or less said that he and Christie had had a love affair, but somehow Eden couldn't believe it. Christie was not a girl—she had been married, and widowed, even though she was still in her mid-twenties. Her taste, obviously, was for mature men. She had married a man many years her senior, and now she was going to marry Sin Watermount. Don was just too immature for her.

Eden's thoughts switched suddenly to herself. 'How mature am I?' she wondered, and she knew she wasn't very mature at all. She hadn't had what you could call a love affair with Berry Addison—it had been no more than in the making, and if she had thought before the break-up that it might develop into something serious, now she knew that it never would have. Berry was good-looking and glib—too glib!—with his tongue, and he had happened to be around when she was lonely, that was all.

The cassette came to an end and Sin went inside to look out some more music. Bibi hissed at Eden, 'Why don't you trot off home now Don's gone, for goodness' sake?'

Eden flushed faintly. 'I'm not ready for bed yet, and I don't think Don wants my company.'

'Don't worry, he'll have gone to bed—and he's not the

only one who doesn't want your company.'

Sin came back then, and Eden settled back in her chair, her hands behind her head, her lashes lowered. Bibi looked ready to kill her as she tossed a big cushion on the ground at Sin's feet and dropped down there, leaning against his knees.

Eden sat on stubbornly, determined not to leave Bibi and Sin here alone, and it was Sin who eventually put an end to the battle of wills when he yawned and said, 'That's about it, girls. Off home to bed now—and make it snappy or you're going to be caught in a downpour. Great for the bananas, Bibi, but no good for pretty hair-dos and terrace skirts.'

'You have the thickest skin of any person I know, Eden Dare,' Bibi said a few minutes later as the two girls went through the short stretch of bush between the two bungalows. 'Surely you know when you're not wanted?'

Eden said dryly, 'I know very well that a man of Sin Watermount's experience is quite capable of arranging things to suit himself, Bibi. If he'd wanted you all on your own, he'd have worked it that way. You forget about Christie, don't you? Just because Sin's kissed you a few times you shouldn't let it give you ideas. Kisses are nothing.'

'What a smug little speech!' said Bibi with a sneer. 'As for kisses, there are kisses *and* kisses, Eden Dare. When it comes to cooking fish you might be able to teach me something, but just don't start thinking you know more about men than I do. You might remember as well that I've known Sin a lot longer than you have.'

They had reached the bungalow and Eden went in ahead of Bibi, and felt Khu Khan's silky coat brush against her legs as he bolted outside. She felt slightly sickened by the conversation, but she said determinedly, 'Then Sin's had plenty of time to make up his mind whether he's seriously interested in you or not, hasn't he? And it's my guess that he's not—that Christie wins from you hands down even if she's not here to prove it.'

'Oh, why don't you push off?' said Bibi rudely.

'If I did,' said Eden wryly, 'you wouldn't be able to stay here, would you?'

'I'd go and stay at Sin's,' Bibi retorted.

Regardless of his work, thought Eden, incensed—because she really thought Bibi would be prepared to make an attempt at doing what she said. With a brief 'Goodnight', she went to her room.

She was in her pyjamas and ready for bed before she remembered that Khu Khan had dashed outside, and now of course it was raining—pouring, rather, in the way it did on this part of the coast. Great for the bananas but—'Damn Sin Watermount!' she thought almost violently. Why did his remarks and opinions have to keep impinging on her thoughts? She stood at the bedroom window and stared out into the soaking darkness of the night. The silver shafts of rain shot down sharp as arrows all ready to drive their shafts into the heart of poor Khu Khan!

No doubt he'd have found shelter somewhere. She would be mad to go out looking for him in such heavy rain. She'd wait till there was a lull and by then he would be only too ready to come in. By then, too, she might be more in the mood for sleep. Right now her whole system seemed to be churned up, her mind and her emotions most of all. She began counting off the days on her fingers. Bibi and Don were only staying about a week—soon they would be gone. And wouldn't it be great if Sin went too? Somehow she no longer felt capable of coping with him on her own—not since he had half flattered, half belittled her, and come so close to kissing her.

As if kisses mattered! Yet as Bibi had said, there were kisses and kisses . . .

The rain stopped almost abruptly, and Eden went quietly

through the house and cautiously opened the front door. There was no bedraggled cat waiting there, and she ventured into the garden. Bibi's room was in darkness, she could see the glow from her own bedroom window and a light shone still from Sin's bungalow. So despite his yawns he had not yet gone to bed. What was he doing? Working again on that book of his that was—what had he said?— 'a particularly masculine type of fiction—a mixture of fact and wild adventure'. Nothing that would interest Eden Dare ...

She suddenly realised that she had reached the end of the garden without so much as calling Khu Khan once. Through the bush she saw a shadow move and her heart jumped before she realised it was Sin Watermount. Moonlight fell eerily through the low fleeing clouds, raindrops glistened on leaf and bush, and the scent of ginger blossom was unbearably beautiful. Eden became aware that she was wearing pyjamas—pale pink cotton, long-legged with a scalloped edge at neck and armhole, and the sight of Sin coming towards her through the trees was having a drastic effect on her nerves and also on her breathing apparatus.

He said when he was near enough, 'I thought that must be you drifting like a ghost through Christie's garden. Here —is this what you're looking for?' He opened his shirt and produced a wretched-looking Khu Khan, with drenched fur.

'Yes,' said Eden faintly. 'I'm—sorry if you've been disturbed.'

He didn't answer that. 'Will he go to you or will we lose him if I attempt to pass him over?'

'He' and 'him', not 'it'. Eden had reached out her arms for the cat when Sin said decidedly, 'You're wearing thin pyjamas and the creature's sopping wet. I'll carry him for you. You'd better give him a good rub down with an old

128

towel when you get inside—Christie keeps such things in the broom cupboard, I believe.'

He sounded so brisk and matter-of-fact Eden was disconcerted, though she hardly knew why. They walked back together to the bungalow, and the cat leaped out of Sin's arms and raced inside through the open door.

Eden laughed a little and said, 'Thank you—we're all right now.' But before she could turn away, he caught her by the shoulders.

'Eden——'

Her eyes widened as she looked up at him, and her heart began to pound. Her lips parted and then—she couldn't think how it happened, but she was in his arms and his lips were about to meet hers——

She jerked herself free and slapped his face. And fled.

Back in the safety of her room she stood shivering, the cat forgotten, hating herself for letting that happen. Not the slap, but what had come before it. And she had appointed herself his guardian! Why couldn't he stay as he had been? she asked herself, anguished. Hard, censorious, suspicious, disapproving—her enemy, with no reservations. She thought of Christie, and—'How can you?' she wanted to ask him. And she wanted to weep. If Bibi had never come here—if she had never seen it as her duty to cling like a leech—none of this could ever, possibly, have happened. She and Sin would have gone on hating each other, and that was the way she liked it. With that she could cope— not with this other thing.

So was she not going to hang on any more; she would keep away from him. He could do what he liked, and so could Bibi. There could be kisses and kisses, but she didn't want to know about them.

In a few days the Websters would go back to the banana plantation, and that would be that. After all, if Sin Water-

129

mount was the type who played around with other women when his fiancée was out of sight, then he was that type, and there was nothing she could do about it except keep out of his way.

Eden raised her eyes and saw herself in the mirror, and discovered that she had bitten on her lip and drawn blood.

In the kitchen she found the miserably wet Khu Khan consoling himself with a few morsels of fish he had left earlier, and she spent ten minutes rubbing him dry with an old towel, which was at least slightly therapeutic for them both.

She felt limp and listless in the morning. Bibi went bouncing off to the beach, and Eden didn't care who she met there or what she did. Don went fishing. Eden sat around in her dressing-gown half the morning, then showered and busied herself with some tidying up. It wasn't fair to let Christie's pretty house get in such a mess. She wondered if things were going well for Amy, and hoped they were. Then she would be able to feel that this endurance test was worth while.

Dusting the living room, she found a drawer in the writing desk half open, and as she shut it she glimpsed the pieces of a sturdy little pot, with a dark sheeny glaze, that usually stood on top. How had that got there? And who had broken it? Bibi? Eden left the pieces on the desk and went in search of the glue, and while she was rummaging in the kitchen drawers, Bibi, followed by Sin, came in through the back door. Bibi was in her green bikini and looking very sexy, and she said a casual 'Hi,' as she passed by Eden. Sin wore white shorts and the towel slung around his neck showed up his brown torso. His thick hair was ruffled and salty-looking, and his green eyes were slightly bloodshot from the sea.

No, Eden thought as he lingered near the kitchen counter, he was really not what she would call good-looking. It

130

was a satisfying thought, yet when he spoke to her she could feel herself going to pieces. She had slapped his face last night and he hadn't forgotten it, and he hadn't forgiven her.

'How's the sensitivity this morning? Are you still ready to act outraged if anyone comes near you?'

'If *you* come near me,' she quipped back, without thinking. 'So I wish you'd stay away.'

'I'm poison, am I?' he asked laconically. 'I thought you'd reached more reasonable conclusions lately.'

'Did you? Well, I'm sorry, but I just don't like you,' she said tightly. She had found the glue and with face averted marched across the living room to the writing desk, and began to examine the broken bits of pottery.

He followed her and perched on the arm of a pink-upholstered chair, looking aggressively masculine against its femininity, with his tanned chest and his muscular legs glistening with bleached-to-golden hairs. Her fingers shook as she examined the fragments of the pot.

'What happened this time?'

She looked up and straight into his eyes half veiled by their thick straight lashes. His lip was curling, and she looked away again quickly.

'I wouldn't know. I found the pieces shoved into the writing desk drawer.'

Sin made no comment, but Eden could feel him watching her as she fiddled about fitting the pieces carefully together, cursing the unsteadiness of her fingers. There didn't seem to be any pieces missing, and forcing herself to concentrate on what she was doing, she set about mending it.

Neither she nor Sin had said anything further when Bibi reappeared wearing a skirt and a bra top. She stopped beside Sin, clasping her hands on his shoulder and leaning against him.

131

'Oh, have you broken something, Eden?' she asked, her brown eyes innocent.

'No,' said Eden flatly. 'As a matter of fact I was going to ask you the same question. I found the pieces hidden away out of sight when I was cleaning up.'

'Well, honestly,' Bibi protested with a hurt look, 'do you think if I broke something by accident I'd hide it away in the writing desk? Christie probably broke it herself—she's got five thumbs on each hand. It doesn't look very valuable, anyhow.'

'It's one of Lorraine's pots,' Sin said briefly. 'As for Christie and her thumbs—you're being uncharitable, Bibi ... Don't waste too much time over it, Eden.' He got up from the arm of the chair and ran long brown fingers through hair that was already rumpled. 'I'd better go and dress. Are you coming with us, Eden? We're going out to lunch—you might like a break from the kitchen. Please yourself, of course. I'll be ready in half an hour.' He pulled Bibi's hair and disappeared, and Bibi told Eden immediately, 'You're not coming. Sin only asked you out of politeness.'

Eden felt irritated beyond all reason. Bibi didn't have to tell her what to do. She wasn't going anywhere Sin Watermount was—she had already made up her mind about that. She—she had washed her hands of him. She told Bibi scathingly, 'Don't worry—I don't enjoy your company all that much.'

'I know that. I thought it was Sin's company you were so desperate for, the way you hung on last night.'

'I hung on because I don't think you're playing fair wth Christie away,' Eden said, managing to keep calm.

Bibi laughed without mirth. 'Now don't give me that line! Didn't you manoeuvre a rendezvous for yourself and Sin on the beach the other night?'

'No, I didn't. It was purely accidental ... now please let me get on with mending this thing you broke.'

132

'I didn't break it,' said Bibi, and stalked off.

'Liar,' thought Eden, and was ashamed of her feeling of viciousness. She applied glue to the last fragment of the pot, but her attention was not wholly on what she was doing. Why had Sin asked her to come to lunch too? She had shown him how she felt about him—and men don't usually go around issuing invitations to girls who slap their faces and admit openly to disliking them. Anyhow, she wasn't going—that was quite definite, and she didn't know why she couldn't put the whole thing out of her mind.

She had just finished her repairing job when a car came up the drive, braked to a stop and disgorged a dark good-looking young man. Bill Hendry, she realised after a moment of startled surprise. She had almost entirely forgotten his existence, and didn't know whether she was pleased to see him or not. He was certainly pleased to see her, for when she went to the door he greeted her with a hearty kiss, asked, 'Where's Amy?' and before she had time to answer added, 'I told you I'd get down the coast to visit you. Are you pleased to see me?'

'Yes, of course,' she said, smiling a little and feeling her spirits lift somewhat. 'Come in, Bill. Amy's not here, as a matter of fact—she's staying with friends down the coast.' She realised that he was looking at someone over her shoulder, and turning her head discovered Bibi there. She made the introductions, and Bibi said, 'Well, you're set now your boy-friend's here, Eden. I'll see you later. Goodbye—er—— Nice to have met you,' and she whisked past them and down the drive—and would proceed to tell Sin Watermount that Eden's boy-friend had turned up, Eden reflected wryly.

She and Bill went out to lunch too, and by a coincidence Sin and Bibi came into the same restaurant. They took a table closer to the door, and Sin sat facing her. Eden felt utterly unnerved. She wished she could have changed places

133

with Bill, but she couldn't think of any sensible reason to give. Afterwards she found she had absolutely no recollection of what she and Bill had talked about. Despite her efforts she simply couldn't keep herself from looking at Sin, but she didn't once catch his eye, and if he had seen her, then he didn't bother mentioning it to Bibi, because quite certainly Bibi would have glanced round. *Was* he so completely wrapped up in Bibi that he didn't see her? Eden just couldn't believe it, and she found it frustrating —more than that, *sickening*—that he wouldn't look at her.

The other two went out, Sin with an arm casually around Bibi's waist, and she tried to forget them; and not much later she and Bill went out to the car he had borrowed for the day and drove away from Burrangarra, where the beach was crowded with summer holidaymakers, and swam at a quieter beach further south. Eden supposed she must have behaved normally—talked and laughed and said the right things—yet no matter how much of an effort she made, she couldn't keep her mind from burning with thoughts of the other two. Where were *they* now? What were they doing? As she lay face down on the hot sand with Bill stretched out at her side, she was tortured by visions of Sin and Bibi in each other's arms.

The afternoon seemed interminable. They ate somewhere around seven o'clock and danced together on a tiny floor, and Bill put his cheek against hers.

'I've been dreaming about doing something like this ever since we dropped you off at the bungalow that day half a century ago,' he told her. 'If you say the word, Eden, I'll leave Murwillumbah and spend the rest of the vacation at Burrangarra, so I can see you every day.'

Eden shook her head, embarrassed, knowing that while his presence might relieve some of the pressure that had built up in her mind, it wouldn't be fair to encourage him. He was a nice man, but she wasn't interested. She wasn't going to let him build up false hopes that would be shattered when they were back in Kamballa.

'No, Bill,' she said decidedly, 'I wouldn't want you to do that.'

'Why not? Is there someone else around?'

'No, of course not,' she said sharply, then wished she had said yes when he bent his head and kissed the side of her neck and observed cheerfully, 'Then there's hope for for me yet ... I'm crazy about you, Eden. I've thought about you the heck of a lot since we met. We just have to get to know each other better. You'll be living with Amy back in Kamballa, will you?'

'I—I don't know,' she said uneasily. 'I have to find a job —I might leave Kamballa altogether.'

'I won't let you,' he murmured, kissing her forehead.

With a jolt, Eden's mind went back to Bibi and Sin. She knew that if Sin were kissing Bibi at this instant it wouldn't be on the forehead or on the side of her neck. Oh, God—— 'Don't think of it,' she told herself desperately. But it was no use, the thoughts went on and on and suddenly she felt utterly, physically sick.

She said abruptly, 'Bill, I've got to go home. I feel—I feel bad——'

He looked at her in consternation. 'You do look crook— you look green! It must have been the oysters. Gosh, I'm sorry, Eden.' He put his arm around her protectively and led her off the tiny dance floor. 'Hadn't we better find a doctor?'

'No. No—please, Bill. I'll be all right if you'll just take me home.' There was perspiration on her forehead and on the palms of her hands, and her head was spinning. But it wasn't the oysters. She knew with a sudden deadly clarity what was making her feel so sick and look so green. The sickness was the sickness of love, and the green was the colour of jealousy—a devouring jealousy that had been

135

gnawing its way through her all afternoon, all evening, and had now, finally, reached her heart.

Sin's bungalow was in darkness when Bill took her home, and so was Christie's, and she refused to let him come in with her. Khu Khan was waiting at the front door and she felt a weak surge of guilt. Poor Khu! He must be ravenous, and she had completely and selfishly forgotten him. She scarcely noticed Bill driving away, but the business of attending to Khu Khan's dinner restored to her some semblance of calmness and sanity. She watched him eat hungrily, yet still fastidiously and with the politest of manners, and then she picked him up and petted him a little and found him completely forgiving and appreciative, despite her omissions.

She switched off the kitchen light and went through to the bedroom, treading softly until she discovered that the open doors of the other two bedrooms revealed that neither Bibi nor Don was home.

So Bibi was still out with Sin. The realisation was like another blow just as she was on the point of recovering her equanimity.

In her own room, Eden shut the door and sat on the edge of the bed in darkness, her hands clasped in a kind of agony. Could it be true that only last night she had pulled herself out of Sin's arms and slapped his face? Oh, God, how could she possibly feel this way about Sin Watermount? It was so illogical—so completely impossible!

She felt the bitter taste of love, unwanted, unrequited, in her mouth. Yes, with anguish she acknowledged that she was hopelessly, *stupidly*, in love with Sin Watermount. That was why she didn't want Bibi running after him. Her concern was not for Christie, but for herself. Sin was right—she was a nitwit. But when had it happened? And how? She thought again of what he had said about the sea, and she knew that she had been carried away out beyond her depth, that she was drowning—drowning——

'*Forget it*,' she told herself sharply, getting up from the bed and groping for the reading light. She felt ten years older than she had been last night. 'Forget it and it will go away.'

But she couldn't forget it and it didn't go away. She lay tense and wakeful in the dark until she heard the sound of Sin's car, the front door opening, the muffled sound of footsteps. And it was not until a long time later that Eden fell into an exhausted sleep.

CHAPTER EIGHT

EDEN was wakened in the morning by Khu Khan jumping on to her bed and touching her face with a gentle paw. With a shock she discovered that the digital clock said ten-thirty-three, and that her room was growing suffocatingly hot.

Except for herself and the cat the house was empty, she learned when she had dragged on a short cotton robe and gone through to the living room. She glanced through the big windows, but in the scintillating blue of the sea she saw no one swimming, and that was no surprise. Sin would have been out of the water hours ago, and she wondered with a sick feeling in her stomach whether he was working or whether he and Bibi were somewhere together—kissing, making love. She turned away from her thoughts with a feeling of revulsion. It seemed that jealousy was a powerful poison, and she knew a vindictive urge to confront Sin—to ask him how he dared to play with the emotions and

137

senses of two girls when he was already seriously involved with Christie Vaughan. The rational part of her mind insisted that in such circumstances she couldn't possibly be in love with him.

And yet she was.

Listlessly, she went into the kitchen and put fresh water in Khu's bowl, tipped some biscuits into his dish, and made herself coffee. She didn't want to eat, she wasn't hungry. Bibi and Don had left their breakfast dishes littering the kitchen, and more for something to keep her occupied than for any other reason, she washed up and swept the floor.

Don's bed had been roughly made, but Christie's big room where Bibi slept was in its usual disorder; the sheets on the double bed were crumpled, the quilt dragged on the floor, and the doll in its nylon lace dress lay head down on the carved sea-chest, amongst a tangle of Bibi's garments. Eden shut the door on it. It all seemed to indicate how little Bibi cared about Christie. She certainly wouldn't let her get in the way if she were seriously determined to win Sin for herself.

'But she won't,' Eden thought. Sin was just fooling around, amusing himself. He would fool around with her too, his behaviour of the other night indicated, if she were willing to let him. Why, she couldn't imagine, seeing they had started off as sworn enemies. Anyhow, for her fooling had had no attractions—and never had had.

She tidied her own room, took a shower and dressed. It was strange how empty the house seemed—empty and forlorn. Even Khu Khan had disappeared, and she wandered outside partly to look for him and partly to glance in the letterbox.

One letter today—and it was for her! From Amy. The sun was fierce, and she walked back inside as she ripped the envelope open with eager fingers. Perhaps Amy was coming to Birrie Point at last, unless she was merely writing with

138

news of the progress of her romance with Malcolm Hewett. In any case, Eden felt rather pathetically comforted to have a letter from her on a day when she was feeling so low-spirited and lonely. Standing in the middle of the living room, she unfolded the pages and began to read.

'Dear Eden—What do you know, I've had a letter from Bangkok, from Christie. I let her know I was here and you were there, so she wrote, and you wouldn't believe it, she's got herself in a terrible mess—that man of hers really should have gone with her, work or no work. She's gone and met some guy—an Australian from Adelaide—and fallen in love with him.'

Eden uttered an involuntary exclamation of disbelief and stopped reading. Oh no! It just couldn't be true of Christie —not almost the minute she was out of sight! And all this time Eden Dare had been conscientiously slaving away protecting Sin Watermount from Bibi!

A slightly shocking thought crowded this one out—If Christie was through with Sin, couldn't there be a chance for poor love-struck Eden? She bit her lip and grimaced. No, she was really going off her head—there never had been a chance, and there never would be.

Shaken, nevertheless, she returned to the letter.

'Hard to believe, but there it is. And it's a fact of life that wherever Christie is, there's always an admiring male or two, and she *is* impressionable and soft-hearted. But I'm positive it won't last—absolutely positive. She'll come home and realise it was just a silly holiday affair. I mean, when you have a man like S.W. waiting for you, it stands to reason, doesn't it? But here's what's bothering me, Eden, and this is why I'm writing. Being Christie, my cousin will have written and confessed the whole thing to Sin. So please, Eden, keep an eye on him. Of course you can't *say* anything—just in case he *hasn't* heard from C.—but if he shows any signs of racing off stricken to S. America or somewhere, *stop him*. I don't care how you do it, so long as he's still there when she comes back. Tell him you're scared stiff all by yourself—anything. I'll probably be joining you soon; anyway, I'll be in touch. Love and thanks, Amy. P.S. I know I'm being selfish leaving it all to you, but I'll probably have great news next time we meet. A.'

Eden read through the letter again feeling slightly dazed. *Had* Christie written a confession to Sin? Certainly he had shown no signs of packing up and disappearing to South America. He hadn't even got as far as Canberra! But— Eden frowned thoughtfully—would a mature man like Sin Watermount react that way? Eden thought not. He would know as well as Amy that Christie would come to her senses. He was so self-assured, so positive, so—so arrogantly male.

He wouldn't make it easy for her, though, even if she came home repentant. 'I wouldn't like to be in Christie's shoes,' Eden told herself with a shudder. He was tough enough when you'd done no more than forget to lock up or accidentally break something.

Quite suddenly, as she stood there staring at nothing, she knew what Sin Watermount was up to. He *had* heard from Christie. Of course he had!—possibly even before Amy. It explained his behaviour perfectly. He was going to frighten Christie with a counter-romance, that was it. That was why he had been flirting so heavily with Bibi.

'But where do I come in?' Eden wondered bleakly. What had been his object in trying to start something with her when Bibi was so obviously a satisfactory foil? Perhaps he thought there was safety—for himself—in numbers, she reflected cynically.

She drew a deep breath and with hands that shook slightly put the letter back into its envelope. While she didn't share Bibi's opinion of her, she had to admit that Christie Vaughan, with her extraordinarily fickle behaviour, had gone way down in her estimation. At least she knew the score now, she thought tiredly, and she quite definitely was not going to be around when Christie came home. Bibi could be there if she wanted to, but Eden would be well and truly missing. Sin wasn't going to have two adoring females at his feet to frighten the erring Christie out of her wits ...

She was aroused from her thoughts by the sound of someone whistling, and she became aware of Don grinning at her from the kitchen and holding up a couple of fish.

'Oh—not *more* fish, Don!' she exclaimed involuntarily, and he grimaced and shrugged.

'I never get sick of fish—besides, I'll be back amongst the bananas soon enough. I caught this lot off the rocks just now. It's pretty fierce there this morning. Sin hasn't had any luck as yet.' There was more than a slight note of triumph in his voice, and while Eden was aware of it, she was still more aware of the effect the very sound of Sin's name had on her physical being. Her stomach seemed to turn over, and she turned her head away from Don as though to hide something.

'Where's Bibi?'

'Lying on the sand. Should be home for lunch soon. Want me to clean this fish or can't you stand the sight of it? You look a bit white around the gills.'

'Oh, I'm all right. Of course we'll eat your fish,' she said with an effort at cheerfulness.

She was preparing a salad and Don was outside cleaning the fish when someone banged on the front door and Sin Watermount's voice called sharply, 'Open up, someone, please!'

Eden's nerves jumped. What was the matter? She dropped the tomato she was slicing and hurried through the house, and when she flung open the door she gaped. Sin stood there, holding in his arms the limp form of Bibi wrapped in a striped surf towel, her hair dark with water, her

141

face white, her eyes closed. Eden's startled eyes flew to Sin's face. If she had imagined her next meeting with him it had been nothing in the least like this.

'She's not drowned,' he said crisply, moving past her. 'Though she came damn near to it. Where does she sleep?'

'Here.' Eden pulled herself together and hurried ahead to open the door of Christie's room, where she started to straighten the crumpled sheets. Sin dumped Bibi's body somewhat unceremoniously on the bed. Under the striped towel she was naked except for that ridiculous wisp of a bikini, and Eden gasped as she saw blood on the freckled white cheek.

'Mine,' said Sin briefly, indicating a gash on one side of his bare chest where the blood had not yet congealed. 'Get a blanket, we'll wrap her in that. She's shocked and consequently cold. Is there such a thing as a hot water bottle around?'

'There's one in the linen closet,' Eden remembered. She opened the chest at the foot of the bed and pulled out a soft pink blanket and helped Sin wrap it round the shivering Bibi, who appeared little more than half conscious. 'Shall I call a doctor, Sin?'

'No need. Her lungs are clear and there's no damage elsewhere. I cut myself on the rocks as I lugged her out of the water. All she needs is a cup of tea with a drop of brandy in it and a few hours of sleep and quiet, and she'll be as good as new.'

He followed Eden out as she went for the hot water bottle, and she asked him quietly, 'How did it happen?'

As she looked at him across her shoulder from the linen closet she discovered his green eyes surveying her, so coldly that she was jolted. Oh, God, what had she done now?

'She would come messing about on the rocks where I was fishing,' Sin said after a second. 'I yelled at her to look out, but it was too late. She was washed off by a thunder-

142

ing great wave she didn't see coming, and I had to fish her out.'

Eden glanced again at the long gash on his chest.

'Shouldn't that be dressed?' she asked.

'Presently,' he said impatiently. 'We'll see to Bibi first. Where's Don?'

'Outside the back door.'

'I'll tell him what's going on. Get that bottle filled and then make some tea, will you?'

She nodded. 'The kettle's been on. It won't take a minute.'

She did as he had said, putting the hot water bottle at Bibi's cold feet and asking her if she was comfortable. Bibi was feeling very sorry for herself. Obviously she'd had a nasty fright.

'Oh, God, I thought I was going to be drowned,' she sniffed. 'Where's Sin?'

'He'll be along,' said Eden calmingly. 'I'm going to bring you some tea and brandy and then you're to have a sleep. You're all right.'

Don had made the tea when she went out to the kitchen, and Sin had gone home to change. Eden poured a cup for Bibi and added a liberal dash of brandy, and Don went in with her when she took it to his sister. He stayed talking to her for a while after Eden left the room and returned to her task in the kitchen, but he had rejoined her with the news that Bibi had gone to sleep before Sin came back.

Sin was wearing a dark shirt and dark cotton pants, and after he had been brought up to date Eden asked him diffidently, aware that he hadn't smiled at her even fractionally, 'What about that cut, Sin?'

'I've already attended to it,' he said dismissingly. 'There's no need for you to worry.'

'Have some lunch with us,' Don invited him, adding awkwardly, 'Thanks for scooping my sister out of the sea. I

143

don't know why she was such a little idiot as to go capering around on the rocks. I warned her about it.'

Sin smiled, not altogether pleasantly. 'Women delight in playing with danger.' He looked at Eden as he spoke, and she wondered if he was thinking of Christie.

After lunch, Eden had started to clear away the dishes when Sin said abruptly, 'Leave that. You can take care of it, can't you, Don? I'm going to take Christie's car for a run and I want Eden to come with me.'

'Sure, I can manage,' said Don affably. 'You go along, Eden.'

Eden's heart had begun to pound. She didn't want to go out in Christie's car with Sin Watermount, and she couldn't imagine why he should want to take her, particularly as he had had nothing but dark unfriendly looks for her today, though she couldn't imagine what she had done to deserve them.

'I'd rather stay and keep an eye on Bibi,' she said with a firmness she didn't feel. 'She might wake up.'

'So what?' said Sin. 'There's nothing wrong with Bibi. Don will be here, so you can quit prevaricating and come along with me.'

There was a look in his eye that intimidated her, and after a second she said shakily, 'All right. If you insist.'

'I do insist. So get yourself ready while I drive the car out.'

Eden went to her room. How weak can you be, she thought resentfully. And yet deep down she knew she wanted to go with Sin, despite all her resolution. 'Women delight in danger,' he had said, and it seemed to be true. But all the danger was for her ...

She brushed her hair, used a lipstick and picked up sunglasses, thinking they would be useful to hide behind. She had the shrinking feeling that today and yesterday had all been a little too much for her. She said goodbye to Don

144

and went down the driveway to where Sin was waiting in the car. He leaned across and opened the door without saying anything, and Eden got in beside him, slammed the door shut, and they roared off.

They drove in silence for several minutes, along the road that led away from Burrangarra. Once or twice she glanced at his profile—hard and masculine and distinctly unfriendly-looking—but he didn't spare her a single look. Even if he was brooding on Christie—and she didn't honestly think he was—he had no right to be taking it out on her, if that was what he was doing. She said after some time, trying to sound calm and rational, 'Look, you asked me to come with you. Do you—do you have to act as if it were my fault Bibi was nearly drowned?'

'I wasn't aware I was doing any such thing,' he said frigidly.

'Then what am I supposed to have done? You keep looking at me as if I'd performed the ultimate in despicable acts. I—I resent it.'

Now he shot her a glance and she shrank from it.

'You think I should look at you as if you were all honey and roses, do you? Well, I don't see you that way. But get it out of your head that it has anything to do with Bibi. It hasn't.'

'Then *what*?' she asked again, her colour, and her voice, rising. 'What's it all in aid of? Are you sour at me because I slapped your face? You asked for it—you knew I didn't want you to touch me.'

She saw a nerve move in his cheek. 'Did I? I'm afraid I don't agree. On the contrary, you practically fell into my arms that night.'

Eden gasped with indignation. 'Fell into your arms! I certainly did not! You—you all but dragged me there.'

He flashed her another glance. 'If I'd dragged you into my arms you'd have known all about it. You wouldn't have escaped unscathed either, Eden Dare. In future, if you want to avoid opportunities for lovemaking, you might keep out of my way. I have very healthy male instincts, as you may discover.'

'I—I want to keep out of your way,' she assured him, though her voice was shaking. 'You're the one who insisted I should come with you in Christie's car.'

'Because I want to talk to you.'

'What—what about?' For a mad moment she thought he was going to confide in her about Christie—even ask her help. But of course he wasn't.

'You told me you'd broken with Berry Addison,' he said after a second. 'Yet you spent half the day—and half the night—with him yesterday.'

'What?' she asked stupidly. She groped in her mind, and came up with the only possible explanation of what he was saying. He had assumed it was Berry she was with yesterday, because he had seen only the back of a dark head. Insanely she wanted to laugh. 'It—it wasn't Berry Addison,' she told him. 'It was someone else.'

He said nothing, but slowed down the car and swung it on to a track that went away from the sea. Fifty yards or so along Sin braked to a stop, and Eden was edgily aware of the silence of the bush all around them as he swung about to face her, stretching his arm along the back of the seat behind her shoulders.

'Is that true? It was your boy-friend, Bibi told me——'

'I can't help what Bibi told you. But she can't have been listening when I introduced her, or she'd have known it wasn't Berry. And—and if you'd spoken to me instead of pretending you didn't see me,' she finished accusingly, 'you'd have known too.'

'Oh, for God's sake, Eden,' he interrupted. 'Did you expect me to sit there smiling at you like an idiot all through lunch while you were to the best of my knowledge complacently enjoying yourself with a man you'd told me you'd put out of your life?'

She listened to him in some bewilderment. What did it matter to Sin Watermount who she lunched or dined with, who she danced with or kissed or whatever? He had Bibi to use as a weapon when Christie came! She flicked a look at him and immediately, suffocatingly, the green depths of his unavoidable, totally masculine eyes drowned and obliterated any equanimity that remained to her. Her heartbeats quickened, and her mind plunged about like a machine out of control.

'So who the hell was it?' he wanted to know. 'You didn't intimate that there was somebody else when you poured out your heart to me the other night, did you?'

'I—I wasn't aware I'd poured out my heart to you,' Eden stammered. She moved uneasily, leaning back against the seat, then straightening jerkily as she felt the shock of his bare forearm against the nape of her neck.

'No? I had a picture of you as a helpless orphan alone in the world, at the mercy of unscrupulous males and hence possibly and understandably wary of anyone of my sex ... So it wasn't Berry Addison. Then who was it?'

He paused, and she said, 'Bill Hendry.'

'And who the devil is Bill Hendry? Can we have a straight answer to that?'

'If you want,' she said stiffly. One would almost have thought, the way he was looking at her, that he was jealous! 'He's a schoolteacher from Kamballa. He's staying with friends in Murwillumbah and he drove down to see me. He——' She stopped abruptly. She didn't have to tell Sin Watermount a single thing about Bill Hendry, and she raised her eyes and returned his concentrated stare with a cold one of her own. 'Is that straight enough? Is there any-

147

thing else you want to know? And if so, would you mind telling me exactly what right you have to pull my life to pieces?'

'No right at all,' he said with a twisted smile. 'Except that I like to put things straight too. And I did happen to tell you on one occasion what I felt about you.'

Eden stared back at him, confused and bewildered. *Were* his eyes cold? They were raking her own, and yet she couldn't interpret the expression in them.

'You think me a nitwit,' she managed with a wry smile.

'I find you too attractive,' he corrected her, his voice hard. 'And I think of you far too much. This morning—when I should have been working—I spent valuable hours fishing off the rocks.'

He didn't say, 'thinking of you', but he implied it—or meant her to think he did. Oh, God, she thought hopelessly, if only it could be true! But she knew better. She knew he was making sure he had plenty of ammunition. The thing was, she wasn't the nitwit he imagined. She told him tautly, 'Now you're wasting more of your time. You were taking Christie's car for a run. Remember?' His face was nerve-rackingly close to hers. She could see every pore, every line, every separate eyelash; the half day's growth of beard on his chin and along his jawline. His eyes drew her own so that what she had said—what either of them had said—no longer seemed to matter, because there was something quite different that their glances communicated. Eden was disturbingly aware of the ambivalence of her attitude towards him, and she couldn't help wondering if he experienced something of the same nature where she was concerned. But it was worse than dangerous to start thinking that way—she would be better off forgetting him——

Even as the thought came to her he turned away, started up the motor, and drove off with a roar.

She sat silent at his side, somehow stunned. Finis. Just like that. Yet what had she expected?

She knew what she had expected—what she had wanted, and she was shatteringly ashamed. For the first time in her life she had the sensation of being fully adult. She felt old, disillusioned, unable to relate to the girl who had left England a few short months ago and suffered under her grandfather's domination; the girl who had found Berry Addison exciting, who had even thought of him as possibly belonging in her future. As for her future now, she couldn't conceive what it was going to be after she left here. It was like nothing so much as a great void, so that mentally she closed her eyes rather than acknowledge that it existed ...

She emerged abruptly from her brief preoccupation to realise that Sin was driving with almost reckless speed along a bumpy track, his nostrils white, a bitter set to his mouth. She tensed nervously and sat rigid, watching the narrow road yet not seeing it, seeing only in her mind's eye the forbidding, saturnine face of the man beside her.

It was almost a relief when he pulled up again, which he did with a suddenness that jerked her to the edge of her seat. Without a word, he flung open the door and got out of the car, turning to ask her cursorily, 'Are you coming?'

Eden hesitated, her nerves on edge, and he added with a tight smile, 'There's something here you might like to see while you're visiting the coast—a *bora*. Or used to be,' he added, frowning abstractedly. 'I haven't been back to look since I was a boy.' He stood waiting and she got out of the car, then walked at his side keeping a couple of feet between them, and looking about her determinedly so as to keep her thoughts strictly impersonal.

As his were, she discovered thankfully, some minutes later when they emerged from the thick forest of eucalypts where bright parrots flew, and cicadas droned out their maddening song of summer. They had reached the edge of a long narrow clearing. On the red earth, twisting away like a snake, was a blurred but deeply incised drawing, in parts vaguely related to the Greek key pattern, then changing to long serpent-like undulations. It was made a secret place by the trees that crowded in on it, their long blue grey leaves hanging down, their edges to the sun. They were shadowy and smokelike, like something seen through the veils of sleep, and beneath them flared the red flames of Christmas Bells.

Eden felt she could almost see the dark naked forms of aborigines flitting through the shadows.

'So it's still here,' Sin said after a long moment. His expression had changed, relaxed, and there was a gleam of pleasure in his eyes that communicated itself to Eden. He reached out an arm and leaned his hand on a tree-trunk that was rigid with thickly carved geometric motifs. 'It must be twenty years since I last came here,' he said thoughtfully, his voice low.

'What—is it?' she asked.

'A *bora*, an initiation ground, the place where the boys were made into men long before white men came to this country. If you listen, you might hear the bellow of the bullroarers, warning the women to keep away, that a secret ritual is about to take place. But you're safe—there's nothing here now but dreams.'

She glanced at him and he smiled slightly and her heart turned over. The sun shone fiercely on his thick hair with its bleached streaks, and everything about him looked so familiar, she felt as if she had known him for ever. She would never be able to forget him—never. She wished that she hadn't rebuffed him a while ago in the car. Even if it all meant nothing to him. If she had been yielding—sympathetic to his mood—he might have taken her in his arms, and this time she wouldn't have slapped his face and run away.

She would have had at any rate one kiss to remember when she went back to Kamballa. And where would be the harm in that? But she had lost her opportunity. Personalities were finished with between her and Sin Watermount. He had brought her to see an ancient *bora* before she left the coast ...

Her lips had parted to ask him to tell her more about the initiation ground when she became aware of a change in his expression, a darkening of his eyes. Quite without warning, he moved towards her and, her mouth still open, Eden stepped back quickly and instinctively. But this time he did what she had protested he had done before. He dragged her remorselessly into his arms, and their contact took her breath away. It was different from anything she had ever experienced. His hands hurt her arms, his lips bruised her mouth, and she was left in no doubt that his passion was aroused.

'Don't——' she managed to murmur as she escaped his mouth for an instant. '*Please*—let me go——'

'Not till I've found out as much about you as you're finding out about me,' he muttered hoarsely.

'What——?' she gasped, but his lips had taken possession of hers again. His hand sought her breast and she struggled against him vainly. Her mind was spinning crazily—there were things she didn't want him to find out about her, things she barely understood herself ... Her body was weakening, and she felt a terrible desire to give in to him. Passion had sprung up like a red rose from a thorny stem, and her whole being was in a fever. His mouth was demanding and his body burned against her own, and woke such fires in Eden that she was a stranger to herself.

Red roses—passion—fire—the sun——

She felt herself go suddenly limp. She was on fire, yet she was cold as ice. Her lungs were drained of air, she was dizzy—fainting——

She didn't faint away completely, but she was conscious that it was only due to Sin's arms holding her up that she didn't fall. He had lifted her bodily, and now she was lying on fallen bark and scented gum leaves on the ground in the shade of a tree, and he was leaning over her. She lay inert, her eyes half closed, a clammy dew on her pallid face, and she heard Sin cursing himself softly as he wiped her forehead, her cheeks, the moisture under her eyelids with a soft linen handkerchief.

When she opened her eyes fully she saw him clearly but with a strange feeling of unreality. Only a moment ago they had been locked together in the sunlight, their bodies all but fused because of some chemistry that she didn't understand—that no one understood. Now his mouth was serious, his green eyes dark as a river, and she who had metaphorically so nearly drowned lay gasping but whole on the shore . . .

She struggled to sit up, her lashes veiling her eyes. 'I'm —sorry.' Her voice was muffled, uncertain.

'*You're* sorry? For God's sake, what do you think I am, then?'

She turned her face away from him. 'It wasn't—your fault. It was the sun. It's so—so hot,' she said huskily, pushing the damp hair back from her forehead. She felt utterly ashamed of what had happened and of her own participation in it. Ashamed above all that it was only the collapse of her body that had saved her from total surrender to a man to whom she was only of passing interest.

'It was *not* the sun, Eden,' he said, his voice low. 'Don't try to excuse me. I took all the breath out of your body. And you let me,' he added. His fingers touched the corner of her mouth, his eyes were intent on hers. 'So didn't we— between us—learn something important about each other?' He smiled faintly in a way that was oddly serious, his face

152

softening, and it went straight to her heart where it hurt the most. 'Next time,' he said in the same soft meditative tone, 'I'll be infinitely more gentle with you.'

Next time. As if she were a willing victim. It was frightening to think of a next time. She had had her kiss, and she had discovered the truth of Bibi's glib, 'There are kisses *and* kisses'. *That* sort of kiss didn't end with the parting of lips. And next time—next time she mightn't save herself by nearly passing out. She would be a very sure candidate for a broken heart when Christie came home and was brought suitably to heel ...

Somehow she got to her feet. She felt shaky, but she faced him squarely. 'I'm not interested in a next time, thank you. We've found out all there is to find out about each other. As far as I'm concerned it's—just a matter of chemistry, and as such it—it doesn't interest me. Now please, can we go home? You haven't forgotten Bibi, have you?' she concluded deliberately.

Sin's eyes, still fixed on hers, went dark again, but with a different kind of darkness, and she turned away abruptly and began to walk quickly through the forest of trees towards the car. She was sitting in the front seat waiting for him when he came, and he got into the driver's seat without a word. He didn't start up the motor at once, and she sat clasping and unclasping her hands, aware that he was studying her, but refusing to meet his glance.

Presently he said with a kind of detached savagery, 'Is your talk of chemistry a calculated insult, Eden Dare?' She didn't answer, but she felt herself trembling, and he continued, 'I'll admit I would never have expected such— sophistry from you. A straight out lie, yes, but not that. Not from a——' he paused and finished coldly and with a deliberation that equalled her own, 'Not from a messy little nymphet with nothing to back her up but one or two liquorice allsorts love affairs ... I'm beginning to wish very much that you'd gone to Murwillumbah with your schoolteacher admirer, and never come here.'

The colour flooded back into Eden's pale face, and in a moment her cheeks were hectic. A messy little nymphet with—— It was all she could do to sit here beside him. That *had* been a calculated insult.

She said fiercely, 'I only wish I could have—the further away from you the better! I—I don't like *your* brand of clever insult. I thought I was supposed to be the one with the uncontrollable tongue.' Tears smarted under her lids but she refused to let them fall, though she couldn't keep her voice steady. 'I came here to help Amy out, you might remember. I didn't come on your account. I didn't ask you to—to make love to me. All along I've wished nothing more than that you should disappear to Canberra——'

'And *that's* a lie,' he said violently. 'You've been *willingly* under my feet. But I might do better than Canberra— a lot better. Would South America be too far away for you?'

Eden blinked. She felt as though she had been struck a blow in the diaphragm. South America! Just as Amy had said. For Christie's sake—or was it for Amy's?—she swallowed down her tears and croaked out, 'Oh no—no, you mustn't go there—that would be mad——'

He laughed shortly. 'I don't think so. I seem to have lost my taste for settling down.'

The next moment he had started up the motor, turned the car round, and they were on their way home.

Eden kept well over to her side of the seat, thinking agitatedly of what Sin had said. She couldn't see how her lack of co-operation could have made him suddenly think of South America. Perhaps it had been in his mind all the time. Perhaps he was consoling himself with her and with Bibi. Perhaps he wasn't nearly so certain of Christie as she had imagined he must be. But should she try to reason with him? She couldn't help thinking that Christie Vaughan didn't really deserve to have people rushing round stopping Sin Watermount from going to South America when she was so busily and unconcernedly falling in love with someone else.

'For all I care,' Eden told herself wearily, 'he can fly off to the other side of the world tomorrow. I just wish he would.'

But that wasn't true and she knew it. In spite of everything.

When at last they reached Christie's bungalow her instinct was to get away from him quickly, but she desisted and made an effort instead to do the right thing. As Sin pulled up in the cool dimness of the garage she said awkwardly, 'Thank you for the drive—and for showing me the *bora*. I shall—remember it. And please, Sin, go on with your book,' she hurried on. 'Don't go to South America. I'm sorry I'm no help to you, but—but Bibi will be up and about again tomorrow,' she finished confusedly.

He stared at her hard, one green eye screwed up. 'What the hell are you talking about?' he demanded. She didn't answer, and after a moment he told her with a wry grimace, 'I apologise for calling you a messy nymphet, etcetera, by the way. You're not a bad kid. The fact would appear to be that our ages set us a long way apart. We don't see things the same way, we want different things ... I won't come in with you. Give Bibi my love.' He spoke lightly, but Eden felt a twist in her heart.

'I'll do that,' she said, and climbed out of the car.

CHAPTER NINE

BIBI was up—dressed—healthy-looking—and in a raging temper when Eden went inside.

'Where have you been, Eden Dare? And where's Sin?' she demanded, standing in the hallway and confronting Eden.

Eden felt slightly sick.

'Sin's gone home. He—he sent his love to you.'

'Well, thank you very much!' Bibi bit out. 'But don't patronise me! You couldn't have asked him to come in, of course. I suppose you told him he shouldn't disturb me or something.'

Eden drew a deep breath. 'Oh, Bibi——'

'Don't oh, Bibi me! Where have you been?'

'For a drive—to take Christie's car for a drive. So the batteries won't go flat,' Eden said, trying to curb her impatience, and feeling that just now she simply couldn't cope with Bibi.

'Don't you drive? Did you have to ask him to take you? —especially this afternoon, while I was lying there practically dead.'

'Don't fool yourself, Bibi,' Eden said tiredly. 'You were asleep. You were no more dead than I am. And taking the car out was Sin's idea, not mine—ask Don if you doubt me.' She attempted to move past, but Bibi blocked the way.

'It was your idea you should go along, I'll bet. You're a jealous cat, Eden Dare. You can't get him to yourself while I'm around, so you go behind my back. Why can't you stick to your own boy-friend?'

'Oh, be quiet, for goodness' sake!' Eden snapped, losing patience. This time she got by and went to her room, where she shut herself in. Bibi and Don could do what they liked about dinner. She wasn't hungry. She was opting out to-night.

She lay on her back on the bed and watched the daylight going, and—of course—thought about Sin Watermount, and what had happened between them at the *bora*. He had changed her life, got under her skin—damaged her life. However you liked to put it. And he had taught her things about herself that she would rather forget. She thought of the long moment he had held her in his arms, her body palpitating against his, the blood pounding in her ears. She felt again the fever of passion burning in her veins, a fever with which she was totally unfamiliar. She remembered how he had kissed and kissed her in that obliterating way ... She knew she would never have had the strength to run away from such urgency, that except for the fact she had almost fainted, something truly drastic would have happened. It was dangerous for her to be alone with him—and it was the last time she would let it happen. She had made resolutions before, but this time she would keep them. Amy had asked her to keep an eye on him. But he wasn't going to rush off to South America. If he really intended going, it would take time to arrange it and in the meantime, Christie would be back and the ball would be in her court. For her part, Eden wished—oh, how she wished!—that she could pack her things tonight and disappear before morning. A quick and painless ending ...

At this point in her reflections, she might have shed a few foolish tears, but for the fact that Khu Khan jumped on to the bed, reminding her that he too wanted to be loved, and that he hadn't had his dinner.

In the morning, Don had packed up all his gear and decided to go back to the banana plantation.

'I've had my break. I've done all the fishing I want to do —seen enough of the surf—bludged around for long enough. I'm going home to help the old man, he needs an extra hand in this heat.'

'Well, I'm not going home yet,' said Bibi. 'I don't want to go back and broil at the plantation—it's not my idea of the good life. That's one advantage in being a woman—you don't have to follow in your father's footsteps, you can escape without being called ungrateful. I'll stay here a while longer. Eden needs company, anyhow,' she finished, sending Eden an insolent smile across the kitchen.

Eden, making the coffee, said nothing. She knew very well that it wasn't on her account Bibi was staying—and no doubt Don knew it too. Actually, however, she didn't want Bibi to go. She dreaded the thought of being left here alone with Sin—of somehow being conned into staying till Christie arrived. She could see it all happening and she knew that it mustn't. So if Bibi would stay——

Soon after breakfast, Don loaded his fishing gear and his luggage into the car—plus some of the fish he had caught off the rocks the day before, and that Eden had stowed away in the freezer. Eden and Bibi went outside to see him off.

'Let's know when you're ready to come home, Bibi,' he told his sister. 'I'll drive down and fetch you.'

'You won't have to. Sin will take me home,' she said carelessly. 'He'll even be able to take Christie's car for a run at the same time,' she added with a malicious look at Eden.

Don said a pleasant goodbye to Eden and was about to get into the car when Sin came sauntering through the bush and up the drive.

'Hello!' His eyes flicked over Eden but didn't linger on her. 'What's going on? Don't tell me you Websters are off back to the ranges already! I was expecting to see you down

158

on the beach later this morning, Bibi. You're not chickening after yesterday's episode, are you?'

'Of course not,' she said with a laugh. She moved closer to him and put a hand on his arm. 'I'll be coming down to the surf. It's only Don who's going. I haven't had nearly enough,' she added provocatively, 'and I haven't even thanked you for saving my life.'

'Oh, you'd have scrambled out,' he said casually. 'The devil looks after his own.' All the same he inclined his head obligingly while she kissed him—on the mouth. Eden turned away, sickened. Sin would never tell Bibi that their ages set them apart, she thought painfully. He might have made a pretty heavy pass at Eden Dare yesterday, but today he was quite obviously prepared to give Bibi all his attention. He had no more than glanced at Eden, and if she had thought he had declared a kind of truce before they parted yesterday, now she was far from sure.

She murmured another goodbye to Don and went back to the house, moving almost blindly in the hot sunshine. How do you cope with jealousy when you have tossed aside even a temporary right to feel jealous? And how do you deal with a love that won't be exorcised, that twists your heart with pain at the very moment you think you have reasoned it out of existence? Sin had no heart, she thought. Yesterday he had intimated that he couldn't get her out of his mind. Today he appeared to have managed it with no trouble at all.

She reached the living room and looked out through the big windows. Don had driven off and Sin stood there with his arm around Bibi's waist. What was he saying to her now? He had already invited her down to the beach. He'd abandoned his work—but not because he couldn't stop thinking about Eden Dare. *Bibi* would have no scruples about taking Christie's place in his arms, and she would think it was permanent. Well, it was Bibi's bad luck if her bubble of happiness was due to burst at any tick of the clock, Eden assured herself. But the thought didn't give her any satisfaction.

She was washing the breakfast dishes when she heard Bibi come in, and ten minutes or so later the other girl appeared wearing one of her minimal bikinis and trailing a surf towel. Her hair—washed of course with Eden's shampoo—was gleaming, and her brown eyes were full of triumph.

'Sin's asked me to go down to the beach. I may be home for lunch but I may not.' She looked Eden straight in the eye. 'We don't want you around—you had your turn yesterday. Now I'm on my feet again, you're unnecessary.'

Eden flushed. She knew that even better than Bibi. All the same she said tartly, 'I thought you told Don you were staying so I'd have company. And don't try to be directive with me,' she added. 'If I want to take a swim at Danger Beach I shall. You don't own the beach any more than you own Sin. And it could be you'll end up just as unnecessary as I am when Christie comes back,' she concluded warningly.

Bibi merely laughed. 'Look whose claws are out! I wonder what happened to *you* yesterday?'

Eden turned away to hide her flushed cheeks, and Bibi walked gaily off.

Eden stared around her vacantly. What next? Vacuum? Dust? Clear out Don's room—see about getting his sheets laundered, and make the bed up? But what was the point? The cleaner was going to fix it all up for Christie.

Eden began to wander restlessly round the bungalow. It didn't take her long to diagnose her trouble. The truth was, she was in agony—jealousy again!—wondering, thinking, about those two on the beach. That lonely beach that was too dangerous to be attractive to holidaymakers.

Finally, shamefully, her tortured mind could stand it no

more. Once more her resolutions were tossed aside as with a helpless feeling she went to her room and got into her swimsuit. She made no excuses, she admitted that she despised herself, but she didn't care. She had to see him. It was as simple as that.

She took her sunglasses, her towel, locked the house and put the key in the pot, and went down to the beach.

Anticlimax.

Bibi was there alone, lying on her stomach facing the sea, her head resting on her arms. The sun burned on her back that was almost bare and already deeply tanned.

Eden stood on the edge of the sand in the shadow of the banksias. Sin wasn't there. He wasn't in the sea. He wasn't fishing from the rocks. He wasn't lying in the sun beside Bibi. Was he working? Or was he making plans for South America? She didn't know, but she could have wept with disappointment. Well, she would have a swim anyhow.

She walked across the sand and tossed her towel and glasses down beside Bibi. She kicked off her sandals and Bibi rolled over on her back and stared at her, then sat up.

'Oh—it's you! I thought it was Sin.' She looked around her. 'Isn't he here yet?'

'What do you think?' Eden said flippantly. 'I'm going to have a swim. Are you coming in?'

'I'm waiting for Sin.' Bibi looked away from Eden, her gaze settling on the sea. Eden looked too, and for a few seconds watched the dazzling sapphire breakers come riding in to open amazingly green jaws before they crashed into foam. Those jaws, she thought—they could swallow you or they could play with you. It wasn't what you'd call a big surf, not really big, and it had a reassuringly orderly look about it. It had been a very high tide, but now it was on the turn. She asked Bibi, 'It's all right to go in, I suppose?'

Bibi's lips parted. Then she said, 'Why not?' She shrugged. 'Sin's coming down later—but he didn't ask you to come. He had enough of you yesterday. Why don't you run away and play by yourself somewhere else?'

Eden had a childish and unworthy impulse to kick sand in her face—which she didn't obey, of course. She was beginning to like Bibi's company less and less, and she certainly didn't relish the idea of sharing the beach with her. Nor was she going meekly home, leaving Bibi monarch of all she surveyed. When Sin came she would be in the water, and he could please himself whether he came and joined her or whether he stayed here with Bibi. And oh, how she would hate herself if he did stay here with Bibi!

Feeling suddenly sick, she started to run down to the edge of the sea. Bibi called out something after her, but she took no notice.

She had been in the sea no longer than five minutes when she discovered it wasn't safe after all. Suddenly she was struggling against a strong rip that had carried her insidiously into the deep water where the sand dropped away. She had no idea how it had happened. She'd been riding in on a wave—quite successfully she had thought—when unexpectedly she was dragged back and back, away from the shore, and her feet could find nothing solid to anchor her again.

She felt completely helpless. The sea was making a plaything of her, and gasping in fear she tried to swim towards the shore, but watery arms pulled her inexorably back in the opposite direction. The beach now looked a long way off. She could see Bibi there, standing up and shading her eyes, watching her. Eden raised her arm as high as she could out of reach of the water and waved it frantically. She opened her mouth to shout for help even though she knew she could not be heard, but before she could utter, a wave crashed over her head. When she emerged spluttering and coughing in a flurry of foam, Bibi had disappeared. 'Thank heaven,' Eden thought in relief, 'she's gone to get help.' She prayed that Sin would come quickly and come soon.

Then the great green mouth of another towering wave yawned over her head and enclosed her, and she was dashed down into the depths. 'This is the end,' she thought. She didn't think she'd ever surface again. Sin would be too late. The sea was tumbling over her and over, her mouth, her eyes and ears were full of sand and salt water, her head and her lungs were bursting. She was close to unconsciousness when she felt herself dumped with brutal force on hard sand. There was a rushing and a roaring in her ears, sunlight in her eyes—air around her . . .

For a long time to breathe at all seemed impossible, and excruciatingly painful. She was alive—but she was going to be sick.

She was sick—neatly and quickly—there on her knees on the hard wet sand. The water surged up and around her, but silkily, wheedlingly, innocently now, as if it had never meant her the least little bit of harm. She felt so weak she wanted to lie down just where she was—and then she saw Sin running across the beach towards her. He was alone, so Bibi must be back at the bungalow, she thought; putting on the kettle, getting out the brandy, turning down the bed. She wanted to laugh but couldn't, and she wasn't—no, she wasn't going to be carried home and put to bed and made to sleep away the rest of the day. That wasn't Eden Dare's object at all.

She got to her feet.

'I'm—perfectly all right,' she heard herself say. She had taken several staggering steps and was now confronting Sin, who stood staring at her frowningly, his hands on his narrow hips. He wore shorts and no shirt, and a thin gold chain gleamed against the darkness of his chest which was rising and falling from his exertions as he hurried to her rescue.

'You needn't have worried,' she told him with an attempt

at a jaunty smile, but her voice sounded weak and uncertain. His green eyes were raking over every bit of her, and she thanked heaven that she was covered by more than a bikini. 'I was—perfectly able to look after myself. I'm—I'm used to the surf here now.'

'Like hell you are! I saw you from my window by mere chance just a second or two before you disappeared. I expected to have to swim out and look for your body instead of discovering you washed up on the beach. You've got a lot of spunk, haven't you? Are you sure you're all right?'

'I'm fine.' She opened her eyes wide and smiled. He smiled too and unexpectedly and briefly hugged her.

He said almost gently, 'You should check before you offer yourself as a victim to the sea. I'd have thought Bibi's accident yesterday would have smartened you up ... Where is Bibi, by the way?'

Eden stared at him in surprise. 'Didn't she—wasn't she—with you?' she finished lamely, realising it was a pointless question, he he had already answered it with his own. She narrowed her eyes against the sunlight and looked across his shoulder towards the place where she had dropped her things. Bibi wasn't there, of course, and there was no other surf towel, no little pile of belongings beside the things Eden had left. Bibi hadn't run to Sin for help. She had just —disappeared.

Eden swallowed hard. Suddenly it seemed a miracle that she was still alive ... She didn't know if Sin had answered her question or not. She said shakily, 'I'll get my towel and go home and get dressed. Thank you for—coming.' She began to walk carefully over the sand and Sin went with her.

He said, 'The sea was merciful to you today, Eden Dare. But never—never, do you hear me—take such a chance again. I really shouldn't like to think of you making a meal for little fishes.'

'No,' she agreed with a smile. She stopped for her towel, and he said sharply, kicking at a long impression in the sand, 'Bibi was here, wasn't she? Weren't you talking to her? Didn't she tell you I'd left strict instructions to keep out of the surf, at least until I came?'

Everything was spinning round in Eden's mind. What *had* Bibi said—apart from telling Eden to go away and play somewhere else? She hadn't said the surf wasn't safe—but she hadn't actually said it wasn't, either. Eden had just got that impression. None of that really mattered, however. The really appalling thing was that Bibi had known Eden was in difficulties—Eden could have sworn it!—and she had simply walked out on her.

That she couldn't tell Sin.

He had taken her towel from her and draped it round her shoulders, the warmth of his hands brushing briefly against her flesh that was still cold despite the heat of the sun. She raised her head and said carefully, 'I thought it looked safe enough. I thought I'd stay on the edge.'

He looked back at her probingly. 'What kind of an answer is that? Didn't Bibi tell you?'

Suddenly with relief she remembered that Bibi had shouted something after her when she had walked away. She hadn't heard what it was, but now she knew it must have been a warning.

'Of course she did,' she told Sin scornfully.

He said no more—though now he *must* think her a nit-wit, she reflected. He insisted on accompanying her back to the bungalow, and frankly she wasn't sorry to have his assistance. She felt weak enough to have collapsed on the steep climb up from the beach without his firm supporting hand under her elbow.

Bibi was in the living room when she went inside, with Sin following a few paces behind. She was stretched out on the pink sofa, still in her bikini, a magazine in her hand, but she sat up and her face flushed a dull red when she saw Sin.

'Were you looking for me on the beach, Sin? Sorry, I had a headache—repercussions from yesterday. I came home for some aspirin.' She spoke jerkily, and rather belatedly showed surprise at Eden's sickly appearance. 'What's happened to *you*? You look a sight!'

Sin's eyebrows made a straight line across his forehead. 'Eden's been battling in the sea. Don't you think your behaviour's been irresponsible, Bibi, to put it mildly?'

Bibi's flush deepened. She closed the magazine and it slid to the floor. 'If Eden's been telling tales on me, they're not true. I told her not to go in—and I thought she was fooling when she started waving her arms about.'

There was a little tense silence. Eden didn't know what to say. Why had Bibi had to mention that?—except of course that she had a guilty conscience. But she should have kept quiet. It was better for Sin not to know—for no one to know. For Eden to pretend that *she* didn't know. She didn't want to stay and hear any more. She had told herself earlier that bed and tea and brandy were not for her, but after all she didn't want to share the day with Sin and Bibi. She left them to it.

She was already in bed when Bibi came to her room some time later with a cup of tea—laced, of course, with brandy, as she presently discovered—and dumped it on the bedside table. She was wearing a skirt and blouse now, her cheeks were still flushed, and she looked as if she might have shed a few tears, though there was nothing chastened in her manner.

'You're a scheming, mean-minded little pommie, Eden Dare! You've been jealous of me from the moment we met, but this is the lowest you've stooped—trying to make Sin believe I'd have watched you drown. I knew you'd be carried in all right, and that's exactly what happened, isn't

166

it? I just thought I'd teach you a lesson—to quit hanging round me and Sin.'

Eden sat up and reached for the tea and sipped it without looking at the other girl, whose words shook her.

'Don't think he finds you the least bit fascinating either,' Bibi hissed. 'I assure you he doesn't. And I've made damned sure he knows you already have a boy-friend, so just watch your step. He won't want you running around him any more.'

Eden felt herself flinch, but she said with quiet reasonableness, 'If Sin doesn't find me fascinating, then there hardly seems any need to make up lies about me, does there? I suppose that's what you've done.'

Bibi didn't answer that, but her eyes were bright with malice and her lip curled. 'You've put a spoke in my wheel —I've put one in yours. We're even.' She moved towards the door. 'I'm leaving here. I can't put up with you for another day—I should have gone with Don. I've asked Sin to drive me home to the plantation. Sleep on what I've said, won't you?'

She flounced to the door and Eden barely had time to utter a dazed, 'Goodbye, Bibi,' when the door had been slammed shut.

Despite the brandy and her fright, it was almost impossible to sleep after that. Eden heard Sin's car leaving, and she lay with her eyes closed and tears on her cheeks. 'Sleep on what I've said.' Bibi's words burned into her brain—'I've made damned sure he knows—he won't want you running around him——' Oh, God, what lies had she told? But it did no good to worry and wonder, and she didn't suppose she'd ever know. In the long run it wouldn't make any difference after all, Eden reminded herself bitterly.

She had more than a suspicion that it had been Sin's idea and not Bibi's to make her departure today. He could be very high-handed when he chose. The prospect of being here alone with him once more filled her with apprehension, and she looked back with longing to the days when there had been that healthy, *peaceful* enmity between them —if enmity could be peaceful. She wished—oh, how she wished!—that Amy would come to the rescue and release her from a situation that had become intolerable.

She slept at last, and when she woke she rose at once. Physically she felt perfectly normal, though mentally and emotionally she was in a turmoil. She made coffee and drank it with Khu Khan purring on her knee, and she wondered again what Bibi had told Sin to put a spoke in her wheel, and if she had elaborated on it during the drive to Nepelle Heights. Well, none of it really mattered, she supposed. In a year from now she would have practically forgotten this isolated period in her life when she had imagined herself in love with Sin Watermount. She would think of it—if she ever thought of it at all—as a holiday affair. Maybe . . .

The telephone interrupted her not very cheerful thoughts, and as she gently tipped Khu Khan off her lap and went to answer it, her spirits lifted. It must be Amy—and she must be coming to Burrangarra at last.

'Hi,' said Amy. 'How are things?'

How were things! This was one of those times you certainly told a white lie!

'Fine,' said Eden, then burst out almost tearfully, 'Oh, Amy, it's so good to hear your voice!'

Amy laughed. 'You sound lonely. What's been happening? I hope S.W. hasn't buzzed off anywhere. You did get my letter? I didn't want to air all that business over the phone.'

'Yes, I got your letter, and he's still here. But the Websters have gone—did I tell you they came to stay for a week? So I am well, rather lonely.'

'Then cheer up, I'm practically on my way. Malcolm goes home the day after tomorrow, so I'll be with you then, about lunchtime. I've had a super time and I'll never cease being grateful to you, Eden. Christie'll be home in a few days—I don't have the exact date, but I want to be there to see that things get sorted out the right way. Meanwhile, look after yourself and be ready with the congratulations— for me and Malc,' Amy added.

'Oh, I'm so glad!' Eden exclaimed. At the back of her mind she was aware of the sound of the door opening and she swallowed nervously. Was it Sin Watermount letting himself in? He must have planted the key. She said rather hastily, 'I'll be seeing you, then. I'm really looking forward to it—it seems just ages. Goodbye for now—and thanks for the call.'

She replaced the receiver and turned round. Sin stood at the door looking at her intently, a contemplative and far from pleasant smile on his face. Eden's heart sank. He had never looked at her in quite that way before, as if she was —oh, she didn't know what. Was it because of the things Bibi had told him, or was she imagining it? She had never been the recipient of overwhelming friendliness from Sin, and that truce she had thought he had called had been a doubtful one however she looked at it.

She smiled, but her lips felt stiff.

'Oh—you're back. Come—come in.'

'No, thanks,' he said crisply. 'This is far enough for me. I beg your pardon for interrupting you—had I thought you'd be up and about I'd have rung the doorbell. I take it you're feeling all right? You don't have a very good colour yet, despite the suntan.' His eyes went over her with a slowness that was almost an insult, and she flushed. She had got into her pink dress for some reason or other, and she wished uneasily now that she had taken time to shower and wash the salt out of her hair, but she had been afraid Sin would turn up before she was dressed.

She said nervily, her wide eyes unconsciously beseeching

him to believe in her, 'I'm all right. I feel great. Are you—are you sure you won't come in and have some coffee?' Now why on earth had she said that when she didn't want to be alone with him, and would far sooner he went home and left her to her own devices? And why was she so—stricken—when he chose to do exactly that?

'I had coffee with the Websters,' he said, raising his eyebrows. 'I presume Bibi told you I was taking her home. It seemed the best thing to do in the circumstances, with you two girls wrangling.'

Eden bit back a retort. It was true, of course. And did he know that it was all over him? He wouldn't believe it, of course, if she told him of her ulterior motive—to keep him safe for Christie. That seemed somehow laughable now.

'Have you got something for your dinner?' he asked after a moment. 'Or shall I——'

'I'm perfectly self-sufficient,' she said, her head up. 'I don't need *any* help—you don't have to worry about me. I won't smash any more ornaments, I'll lock the doors, and I'll keep well away from your beach. You won't have to keep watch from your window, or—or come up here checking. You can get on with your work or do your research or——'

'That's enough!' he said sharply, as though she were becoming hysterical, and truth to tell she wasn't far off it.

Eden bit her lip. 'And Amy will be here soon,' she said more quietly. 'And so will Christie,' she thought, 'and I shall be gone.'

He nodded, almost as if he knew what she was thinking. 'We've had—quite a time, you and I, haven't we, Eden Dare?' He leaned back against the wall and looked at her through slitted green eyes. 'Getting to know each other. Once we were wound up we really got going, didn't we? It's a pity it was mere chemistry.'

Her cheeks, that had paled again, slowly crimsoned. 'I haven't the least idea what you're talking about.'

'You forget quickly, do you?'

'I—no——' she stammered, badly disturbed by the way he was looking at her. A crazy picture came into her mind, of Sin moving slowly forward—taking her gently in his arms—kissing her——

He pushed his broad shoulders away from the wall and moved fractionally in the direction of the hallway. Then he changed his mind. But her mental picture had been quite wrong—he didn't come slowly towards her—he was there before she knew it had happened, and she was in his arms, pressed close against his body, and his arms were as savage as his kiss.

He let her go suddenly. 'Count that as a final and fare-well kiss, Eden Dare!' she heard him mutter.

In two seconds the door slammed shut behind him. Eden stood where she was, her hand against her bruised mouth, her eyes full of tears.

Why?

In the morning she saw him swimming in the sea, and she did a thing she hadn't done since her second day here. She picked up Christie's field glasses and watched him through them.

And a lot of good it did her, she realised presently. She couldn't see into his mind however hard she looked. He wouldn't be thinking of her anyhow, or if he did, it wouldn't be flatteringly. He wouldn't have a new girl-friend to flaunt when Christie came back after all, but to Eden's mind that didn't matter a fig. 'If I were Christie——' she thought. Oh yes, if she were Christie she'd drop any new boy-friend, however fascinating, the moment she set eyes on Sin Watermount. She could just see it happening—with Christie in the leading role, of course. Not Eden Dare.

She put the glasses away and decided on a day out. For one thing, she had to get away from here or she would be knocking on Sin Watermount's door on any pretext at all. Or on none. And that was only asking for heartache. For another thing, and this was where Eden Dare showed up as being clued up and down-to-earth after all, she wanted to find out how she could get back to Kamballa—tomorrow, or the day after that at the latest. So she wouldn't be here to see Christie throwing her arms around Sin's neck and sobbing out her repentance.

She still had the bicycle, and by nine o'clock she was in the town. By nine-fifteen she'd found a little travel place, and there she discovered that transport in Australia, even on the east coast, isn't always a snip. To get to Kamballa, without the use of a private car, she would have to take a bus down the coast to Coff's Harbour. From there, there was a bus service to Kamballa. The trouble was, it was only a weekly service, and as a bus had left today she would have a long wait. Too long, in fact, to be of any use to her.

Eden felt she simply wanted to lie down and die. Sunbathing was the nearest thing to that, but nevertheless the day was interminable. She didn't want to make new friends, though she could have, and by mid-afternoon she was cycling home, hating herself because all she could think of was that when she got back to the bungalow, she just might see Sin. 'I'll ask him exactly what he meant by that final—farewell kiss,' she thought confusedly, and unexpectedly remembered he had once said that every time she opened her mouth she was asking for trouble.

When she reached the driveway, there was a moke parked there.

A moke! Berry! Oh no, that would be too much. Eden's heart sank as she put the bicycle in the garage. She did a circuit of the house but encountered no one, so he must have gone down to the beach. But what was Berry doing here? How could he have the hide to come and seek her out after the mean way he had behaved? Though it was funny,

172

but looking back now all that business at Overlooking seemed petty in the extreme. She had been so indignant, so angry, at the time. She had decided practically on the spot, with no sign of heartache, that she was through with Berry. Now she wondered what she had been so worked up about. Mainly, if she were truthful, she thought she hadn't liked being made to look so small in the eyes of a stranger. Sinclair Watermount ...

She had hunted in the green pot for the key for several seconds when she discovered the door was open a crack, and her heart had given a leap of fright before she realised what had happened. Berry had found the key. Of course, he would have. Biting her lip in vexation, she went inside and discovered him in the sitting room, asleep on the sofa. She stood looking at him exasperatedly, wishing him anywhere but here. That good-looking face, that dark hair, the permanently crooked eyebrow—she had been quite in love with him once, but how superficially—and how long ago! And just now she had enough problems without having him bothering her. What on earth did he want?

He opened his eyes and looked straight at her.

'Hello!' He swung his legs to the floor and grinned and sat up. 'Surprised to see me, Eden? I hope I didn't give you a fright. You didn't appear to be around, so I used my head and found the key—it was in a fairly predictable place. I didn't think you'd mind me making myself at home. We're old friends, aren't we?'

'I'm not sure about that,' she said coolly. 'We *were* friends, but——' She shrugged and perched on the arm of a chair and looked at him curiously. She just didn't have any strong feelings about him one way or the other. He was weak, but harmless, that was all.

'Were? Oh, come on, Eden,' he said persuasively. 'You're not still cranky with me, are you? I'll admit it was a bit hard on you landing you in trouble like I did, but it blew over, didn't it? I kept away till I reckoned the air would have cleared a bit, then when I rang, some old sheila answered the phone and said you'd gone away. So I called in at Amy's flat. Nobody there, but the folk downstairs gave me the story. So today—I was free—I hopped in the moke and here I am!'

'Well, you can't stay here, Berry,' she said decidedly, 'Amy's not here, and besides—well, you can't stay, that's all.'

'Oh, now listen,' he said, sounding wounded, 'don't hold the past against me. I've turned over a new leaf! And I don't want to stay here. I wouldn't do that to you. I'm booked in at the motel. Now how about a cup of coffee and we can talk things over?'

'All right,' said Eden after a moment. Talking things over wasn't going to get Berry anywhere, as he would soon find out, but giving him a cup of coffee wasn't going to do anyone any harm. Sin was sure to have seen the moke by now. What must *he* be thinking? she wondered as she made the coffee. She felt deeply depressed, but there was nothing she could do about it. Berry was here, the moke was here, the damage had been done. If she were honest, she had to admit that the damage had been done long ago. Sin's opinion of her had never risen more than a couple of degrees, and lately—well, lately it had fallen to well below zero.

She drew a deep and quivering sigh as she poured the coffee, and then, out of the blue, a bright idea came to her.

Why shouldn't she ask Berry to drive her back to Kamballa? She could go tomorrow—as soon as Amy arrived. Oh, if only he would! It was the perfect solution to her dilemma. All this nerve-racking preoccupation with Sin Watermount would be ended, and she wouldn't be here when Christie arrived and Amy was making sure that everything went as it should.

174

CHAPTER TEN

EDEN saw Sin Watermount drive past, no doubt on his way out for the evening, as she carried the coffee in to the living room. To her intense annoyance, her heart immediately began to beat abnormally fast. Why couldn't she just disregard him? she asked herself desperately. This way, she was fast becoming neurotic. Certainly the sooner she got away the better.

'When are you going back to Kamballa, Berry?' she asked abruptly, handing him his cup.

'Well,' he said slowly, as he took it and raised his eyes to her face, 'that rather depends on you.'

'On me? Don't be absurd. How can it?' Eden sat down and crossed her legs, and regarded him coolly.

'Well,' he said again, 'I thought you and I might link up. Actually I've left my job at the bookshop, and I'm considering trying my luck in Brisbane. How would you feel about coming up there too?'

She stared at him incredulously. 'You must be out of your mind,' she said at once. 'I wouldn't even consider it. How can you even ask me, Berry?'

He raised his one crooked eyebrow. 'Because I'm pretty keen on you, that's how. You're the only girl I ever met that I could imagine teaming up with permanently. Come on, Eden—don't hold the past against me, that's not like you. I'm not pressing you to make up your mind on the spot, anyhow. You'll want to go back to your grandfather's place after you leave here.'

She shook her head. 'I shan't be going back to Overlooking Berry. Not ever.'

'What? Why on earth not? I reckon you must be crazy! Good lord, the paintings in that little gallery must be worth a small fortune, and as well the old chap's got a load of stuff that's not for sale—his private collection, you said when you showed me. Aren't you his only close relative, too?'

'Yes,' she admitted slowly. She was beginning to see some reason for Berry's eagerness to team up with her. She gave him a level look. 'Actually I have no choice about going back, anyhow. If you must know, my grandfather tipped me out.'

Berry gave an exclamation of disbelief. 'Not because of me? Good God, I never thought he'd take it all that seriously.' He frowned over his coffee and then brightened. 'Look, you take my advice and go back and call on him, Eden. Hug him—have a cry—you know the sort of thing. He'll soon soften up.'

'I doubt it,' she said with a wry smile. Berry hadn't a notion how self-righteous the King of Diamonds was! But now, surely, was the time to make her request, so she added deliberately, 'Still, who knows? Amy's arriving some time tomorrow morning. I wonder'—she widened her eyes, knowing she was misleading him—'could you take me back to Kamballa tomorrow, please, Berry? I suppose I've been away long enough.'

'Sure,' he said agreeably, and smiled back at her. 'You make the arrangements, I'll fit in with them. And ten to one you'll find I'm right.'

It was as easily settled as that. Eden felt elated, yet at the same time unutterably depressed. There was no going back on her decision now. This was one resolution she would have to stick to. She had burned her boats.

When Berry asked her to have dinner with him she said yes, and he took her to the Silver Prawn of all places. For him, she supposed, it was a sort of celebration.

She arranged for him to pick her up at the bungalow about two o'clock the following day, and asked him not to bother her in the morning as she'd be busy tidying up and packing. Amy would be surprised that she was leaving so soon, but that couldn't be helped, and it would be as well that they'd have little time to talk. During a wakeful night she heard Sin return, and when she rose in the morning she saw him in the sea. For him, life went on as usual. For Eden——

She tried to keep her mind on what she was doing as she restored Christie's room to order from the mess Bibi had left it in, yet all the time she was half expecting Sin to call in, and she felt a nervous wreck. He didn't come, of course—why should he?—and she did her packing and worried a little over what she was going to tell Amy, who for sure would be disappointed to find that she was disappearing the moment she arrived. Anxiety over finding work would have to be her excuse, and she hoped she could make it convincing. She checked up on Khu Khan's supply of steak and found it adequate, and then for some reason she thought to look in the Chinese vase at the wad of notes Christie had left. It looked—different somehow, but that must be her imagination.

Yet when she counted it, she reckoned it must be about fifty or sixty dollars short, allowing for the small amount she had used while Bibi and Don were there. 'Who on earth——?' she wondered aloud, quite badly upset. Not Bibi or Don—*Berry*, of course. Oh, God! so they had dined out in style last night at Christie's expense. Mentally she amended her opinion of Berry. Weak—yes. But not so harmless ... It didn't comfort her that Sin had said Christie would have no idea how much money she had left. She went to her room and rummaged in her handbag, and resolutely put all she possessed, except ten dollars, back in the vase.

177

Now she *would* have to get a job quickly. Her situation was quite desperate. She would really have something to think about when she got back to Kamballa!

Amy didn't come, and at noon Eden went outside to water the garden, and Khu Khan, lying in the shade, watched her lazily, flicking his tail occasionally to show he was awake. In her heart she knew she was hoping Sin would see her and come and speak to her. She didn't care what he had to say so long as she could see him once more. But if he saw her, he wasn't interested and he left her strictly alone.

At one she gave up waiting for Amy, and listlessly lunched alone on a slice of bread and cheese and a cup of tea. Berry was there a little before two, and Eden had to stifle an impulse to tell him she wasn't coming because Amy hadn't turned up. Instead, she scribbled a note for Amy while Berry carried her luggage out to the moke, then she locked the door and put the key in the pot.

And weakened at the last moment.

'I—I'd better slip down and tell my—neighbour that I'm going, just in case anything happens,' she told Berry guiltily.

Sin, bare-chested, was sitting on the patio alone. He was smoking, which he didn't often do, and though there was a notebook on the table at his elbow, he was staring aimlessly into space. Thinking of Christie? Eden wondered, a pain in her heart.

He hadn't looked round at her and she had no idea if he knew she was there or not. She watched him for a few searing seconds, then said, her voice low and uncertain, 'Sin——'

He turned his head.

'Well?' he asked coldly.

'I—I came to tell you I'm going. Amy will be here soon, so——'

'So the conditions won't be right for the pursuit of love, is that it?' His voice was savage. 'Where are you going? Not, I take it, to Murwillumbah. That might cause some confusion, mightn't it?'

Eden listened in bewilderment, not able to make head or tail of what he was saying. 'I—I don't know what you mean. I'm going to Kamballa—to Amy's flat. I have to find a job——'

His eyebrows rose cynically and the coldness of his green eyes almost killed her. 'Such wide and innocent eyes! But you have a tongue, Eden Dare, that the devil would envy. I should never have trusted it. When I walked in on your telephone conversation a couple of evenings ago I was naïve enough to believe you were talking to the schoolmaster you'd—entertained recently. Though not as discreetly as you imagined, by the way. Somebody happened to see his car hidden away in the bush ... I'll admit I'm surprised to find it's now Berry Addison's turn.'

Eden's heart thudded painfully. Her cheeks were now hot, now deadly cold as she realised what Bibi must have told him. Hideous, malicious lies—yet he had believed them!

She breathed out, 'How can you believe such things! Bibi told you, of course—and it's a lot of lies. Can't you see?' Her voice broke, but he said nothing and she stammered on wildly, 'All Berry's doing is taking me back to Kamballa. And that's—that's the simple truth.'

He shrugged carelessly, but she saw a nerve move at the side of his mouth. 'I didn't think you knew what "simple truth" is. You assured me—and on more than one occasion—that you were through with Berry Addison, that you'd never been in collusion with him. Now he spends long hours in the bungalow with you, and the next thing you're careering off to Kamballa—to Amy's empty flat— with him. How do you explain that? What's wrong with

179

staying on here and going back later with Amy?'

That, of course, was a practically unanswerable question. But now Eden had changed her mind about Sin Watermount. Now she *really* knew what he thought of her, and she stammered out on a burst of anger that hovered on the edge of tears, 'What's wrong with it is that I just can't wait to get away from you and your nasty suspicious mind, Sin Watermount. At least Berry doesn't think I'm some kind of poisonous little snake who—who——' She stopped, unable to go on.

'Then run along with him,' Sin snapped. 'We've already said goodbye. Go, for God's sake—and get it over with.'

Eden stared into his eyes for a last moment. 'Gladly,' she said through clenched teeth. She turned her back on him and ran back through the garden. It was only pride that stopped her from bursting into tears. Sin Watermount was the most hateful man she had ever met!

She hated him all the way back over the ranges and across the tableland to Kamballa. She hated him so much that very little of Berry's pep-talk about making it up with her grandfather, and later coming to Brisbane with him, got through to her brain. She even forgot to ask him about the money that had been missing from the Chinese vase, though she had made up her mind to let him know she was aware of the theft whether he admitted to it or not. When they reached Amy's flat, she got the key from the people on the ground floor, allowed Berry to carry her luggage up the stairs, then said goodbye and thank you, but didn't ask him in. He said he'd ring soon and find out how she'd made out with the old man, and she nodded and let it go. She didn't think she owed Berry a great deal of consideration, one way and another.

Once she'd shut the door on him she indulged in a bout of weeping, from which she emerged no longer sure whether she hated Sin Watermount or not, but too exhausted to analyse her emotions. She opened windows and aired the flat, which was unbearably hot, unpacked her clothes, then found a tin of sweet corn and some whole-meal crackers, and made herself a meal.

Amy telephoned, disappointed that she had arrived late and found Eden gone, but accepting her explanation that she was anxious to find herself a job. Amy too was eager to come back to Kamballa, to be nearer Malc.

'As soon as all the business here is settled—you know what I mean, Eden—I'll be home.'

Eden longed to ask about Sin Watermount, but as Amy didn't mention him she didn't either, and when she had hung up she decided to ring her grandfather. Not as a result of Berry's exhortations, but from a sense of duty—to let him know she was back.

He was remarkably affable.

'Ah, Eden, so you've returned. I'm glad to hear from you. I've been—er—thinking over things, and I feel I may have misjudged you. You may or may not be aware of it, but that scoundrel Addison has been in trouble at the book-shop and has lost his job there. I sincerely hope you don't plan to have anything more to do with him.'

'No, Grandpa,' said Eden, smiling wryly to herself. So that was why Berry left his job and was off to Brisbane!

'Under the circumstances,' the King of Diamonds continued pompously, 'I am willing to give you the benefit of the doubt—no, I shall go further than that and forget entirely the unpleasant incident that caused me to dismiss you. You may, in fact, return to Overlooking, Eden.'

Eden could hardly believe her ears. He was certainly stepping down, even if he did make it sound as if she were some rather lowly sort of employee. 'Thank you, Grand-father,' she said ironically, and as she spoke it flashed through her mind that it would be very easy to go back to her grandfather's house—it would, in fact, be like going to a retreat. There would be no more worry about finding work, or thinking of the ten dollars that were all she had left. Perhaps——

'I told you when you went that you would find it hard to obtain a position,' he continued sanctimoniously. 'You evaded the issue by running away to enjoy yourself at the coast, but I predict you will face the same difficulty now. If you're wise, you will accept my forgiveness, and in future be rather more appreciative of the benefits that accrue from living at Overlooking.'

The benefits of being an unpaid housekeeper, Eden remembered, and with little chance of adding much to her ten dollars either. It was all there in his voice to warn her—the arrogance, the I-told-you-so attitude, the mention of her accepting his forgiveness rather than the offer of an apology for wronging her. Quite decidedly if she went back it would be on his terms. Well, she wasn't going to be victimised again, so—— 'I'm sorry, Grandfather,' she told him politely. 'It's nice of you to tell me I'm—absolved, but I don't want to come back. I'd rather be independent.'

'I'm a wealthy man, Eden,' he reminded her sharply, and she could hear the displeasure in his voice, 'and you are my only relative.'

Berry had already reminded her of that, but it was no use.

'I'm sorry,' she said again. 'I just don't feel we—understand each other well enough. I'll call in and see you one day, though,' she promised.

But he was too displeased with her to be interested in that, and dismissively he wished her goodnight and hung up.

Oh well, thought Eden wryly, even if it had to be Hot Chooks and Take-Away Tucker, it would be preferable to being pushed around in her grandfather's home.

For the next two days she tried, completely without success, to find work, but there seemed to be absolutely nothing offering that she could do. Berry rang to ask what she was doing and had she contacted her grandfather, and when he learned there was to be no grand reconciliation his interest in Eden dropped noticeably. Not that it worried her. She was far more concerned with the way her money was disappearing, however frugally she ate. Perhaps she should have stayed on at the coast. But no—coming away quickly had been the only possible thing to do. She only wished the time would come when she would no longer be haunted by that mental image of Sin Watermount, his green eyes so cold, his voice so harsh. How could you even imagine you were still in love with a man who had such a poor opinion of your character?

On the third morning, she decided to try the Martins' handicrafts shop again, and miraculously, she was in luck! Yes, they told her, they were interested. Handicrafts were suddenly booming, they had found it impossible for either of them to take a holiday as there was far too much for one woman to handle alone. They had talked it all over only yesterday, and decided they could afford a junior assistant, and there was to be an advertisement in the local paper tomorrow.

'So you're our very first applicant,' beamed the elder Miss Martin.

Meanwhile there were customers needing attention, and Eden was asked to come back at five-thirty when they'd closed up and would be able to talk to her and decide if she was suitable. Eden left the shop with a tremendous feeling of relief. She was sure she would get the job! She had been on the point of reaching the depressing conclusion that she would have to eat humble pie and go to her grandfather.

Her elation carried her through the rest of the morning. She window-shopped, then bought some bread and a few necessities and went back to the flat. There her high spirits collapsed and she sank into a fit of depression the cause of which she knew very well though she wouldn't admit it to herself. It was only the thought of going back for that interview at five-thirty that kept her from going under completely, and she was determinedly vacuuming the flat—which didn't really need it—when the front door opened and Amy walked in, with Khu Khan in her arms.

The sight of Amy's pert round face and curly hair and sparkling hazel eyes made Eden almost weep with joy; it was all so totally unexpected. The two girls hugged each other. Khu Khan, who had jumped from Amy's arms the minute the front door closed behind her, began rather warily to inspect the flat, and Amy and Eden went to the kitchen to make a pot of tea.

'It's a must,' Amy said, laughing. 'There's so much to tell you and I can't even begin without a cup of tea. Christie——' she began, and then stopped maddeningly as she opened the cupboard to get out cups and saucers and a packet of biscuits.

'Christie what?' asked Eden nervously, but instead of answering, Amy turned and frowned and stared at her and asked suddenly, 'Eden, what's all this about you and Berry Addison? After the way he behaved you can't have—well, you never were seriously involved with him anyway, were you? So why did you run off with him like that? I mean—well, a few days wouldn't make all that difference, and then Sin Watermount said——'

'What?' asked Eden in a voice that was quite expressionless, though she knew the colour had fled from her face. Sin would say anything about her. They—hated each other equally.

'Oh, I don't know,' Amy said uncomfortably. 'He seemed to have the idea that you were pretty heavily involved with Berry—or I guessed it must be Berry—and I couldn't think what could have given him that idea.' She paused, and Eden swallowed but found she couldn't speak. 'Anyhow,' said

Amy, cheerful again, 'I told him if he had any funny ideas about your character, he could go and jump in the sea, because I know you a whole lot better than he ever will. So that fixed *him*,' she finished conclusively.

'Thank you,' said Eden, managing a smile. 'Of course I'm not interested in Berry. I expect Bibi invented a few tales, that's all,' she improvised, letting Bibi down lightly. 'It doesn't matter now, anyhow. I didn't invite Berry over to the coast—he just turned up, so I decided to come back to Kamballa with him. I didn't fancy being in the way while Christie and Sin were sorting themselves out.'

'Fair enough,' said Amy. 'But the way things happened you might just as well have stayed put. There was no sorting out.' She had made the tea and now she carried the tray through to the sitting room where Khu Khan had already appropriated a comfortable chair. Eden sank rather tremblingly into another while Amy poured the tea.

'What do you mean?' she asked after a second.

Amy gave her a wry, half comical look. 'Nobody turned up. Lorraine and her boy-friend went straight to Sydney, and Christie's on her way to Adelaide with Ralph—this man she met. It's serious and they're going to be married fairly soon.'

'Oh no!' Eden exclaimed, her head spinning. 'Poor Sin,' she added slowly, and reflected that it sounded quite extraordinary. Fancy being sorry for a man as tough and hard as Sin!

'Poor Sin nothing!' Amy retorted. 'In my opinion, it serves him right.'

Eden thought she couldn't be hearing aright. Amy speaking like this about Christie's dreamboat—that gorgeous male, Sin Watermount! Yet, when she came to think of it—Amy *would* take Christie's side.

'He did ask for it, you know.' Amy leaned over to stroke Khu Khan. 'It must have really hurt poor Christie's feelings when he suddenly backed out of going to Bangkok, when it had been his idea in the first place. It wasn't what you'd call a chivalrous way to behave, was it? Especially when you consider he hasn't even done any of the research Christie said was his excuse—much less finished his famous book.'

Eden felt guilty. It was her fault, at first anyhow, that he hadn't gone to Canberra. And she had interfered with his work. She and Bibi, she thought. But she couldn't confess any of this to Amy, so she held her peace.

'Anyhow, Sin and I both had letters from Christie, and she asked me to look after Khu. She sent me a photograph of Ralph too, very mature, Christie does like mature men—and he looks really kind and understanding. I'm sure he'll make her terrifically happy.' She dashed off to her room to fetch the photograph, and Eden leaned back in her chair and thought about Sin. What would he do now? In a way, she was glad she hadn't been there to witness his reaction to Christie's news. She felt an ache in her heart that was not all for him. The better part of it was for Eden Dare.

When Amy brought the snapshot, she saw that Ralph was mature indeed. In fact, he was middle-aged—years older than Sin. And yes, his face did look kind. Eden had a clear mental image of Sin's face. No one would describe it as kind—except when he smiled. But how could Christie possibly prefer Ralph to Sin? It just didn't make sense. She asked as casually as she could, 'How did Sin take it?'

Amy shrugged. 'I wouldn't really know. Men aren't exactly communicative about that sort of thing, are they? They keep a stiff upper lip, I suppose. All the same, he was—well, pretty moody. He shot off somewhere. At least, he was just about packed up when I left. I didn't ask questions. He's just a bit awe-inspiring somehow, isn't he?'

Was he? Eden didn't answer that one. Amy would have a fit if she knew some of the things she had said to Sin. 'Every time you open your mouth you ask for trouble,' he'd told her. That was the night he'd first tried to kiss her—the night, she knew now, that she'd begun to fall in love with him, despite the fact he was out of reach. 'You don't know where he was going?' she asked Amy, and there was a tremor in her voice. 'Not—not to South America?'

Amy laughed and made a comic face. 'I hardly think so. To Canberra, probably, to get on with his work.'

Or to Adelaide, thought Eden, to persuade Christie to change her mind. It shouldn't be hard, and it wasn't too late. Christie wasn't married yet.

'I haven't told you the really big news yet,' Amy said after a moment. 'Malc and I are going to be married as soon as Mummy and Daddy come home!'

'Oh, marvellous!' Eden exclaimed. 'I'm so glad for you, Amy. I hope you'll be very happy.'

'I'm sure we shall. And now what about you? How's the job-hunting?'

'Oh!' Eden exclaimed, her eyes flying to the electric wall clock. It was just about five-twenty. 'I have an interview in ten minutes—at the handicrafts shop. I'll just make it.'

'Shall I drive you?' offered Amy.

'Don't bother. It won't matter if I'm a few minutes late.' She hastened away to tidy up her appearance before she went quickly down the stairs. As she walked along the street and turned the corner she wasn't thinking of the interview ahead of her. She was thinking of Sin Watermount, and wondering whether Christie really was going to marry that kind-looking man in the photograph. Perhaps she was piqued and was bringing Sin to heel—which wouldn't be very kind to Ralph.

Eden tried to imagine Sin being brought to heel. He would have to be really crazy about Christie to go to Adelaide and plead for himself, but in her mind she was certain that that was where he had gone. Only he wouldn't

187

plead—no, he would simply drag her into his arms, and Eden knew only too well the effect *that* could have!

She reached the handicrafts shop and rapped sharply on the door. It was closed, but the Martins wouldn't have gone yet; they would be expecting her, and she knew from her own experience that there were numerous things to be done after the doors were closed, before one could go home. In all probability too, they lived in the flat above. She stepped back a little on the footpath, staring upwards—and someone grabbed her by the arm.

'Oh, I'm sorry!' she exclaimed. And turned to find herself looking into the blue-green eyes of Sin Watermount.

She thought her legs would give way, and she went white to the lips. 'Aren't you—aren't you in Adelaide?' she asked faintly, and realised as she said it what a stupid question it was to ask, and in any case, Adelaide was hundreds and hundreds of miles away.

'Now what would I be doing in Adelaide, Eden?' he asked, still holding her arm. His eyes were exploring hers and his mouth was smiling in a very serious kind of way, and she felt she would willingly die at this moment, with him looking at her like that—not in the least coldly.

Behind her, the door of the shop opened, and one of the Miss Martins said cordially, 'Come along in, Miss Dare.'

Eden uttered a small exclamation as if she'd been wakened from a dream and made to step away from Sin, but he wouldn't let her go. He said quickly and authoritatively, 'I'm sorry, ma'am—Miss Dare isn't interested in the position after all.'

'Oh.' Miss Martin stared at him and then she looked inquiringly at Eden, who opened her mouth but hadn't found anything to say when she discovered Sin was propelling her across the footpath. The next thing she knew she was sitting beside him in a car that was decidedly dusty, but recognisable as Sin's.

'Why did you say that?' she demanded, though her voice was husky. 'I—I *am* interested. I have to work——'

'Not if you marry me.'

Eden leaned back suddenly in the seat. He couldn't have said that. She'd imagined it! She was going mad.

He was looking at her, but she refused to raise her eyes.

'I have to talk to you, Eden. When I've finished, if you still want to come back to the Misses Martin, I shall bring you. Is that all right?'

Eden swallowed, and nodded.

He started up the motor and drove off, turning from the main street into a road that led out of town. Then he said soberly, 'I want to beg your pardon for my unforgivable behaviour last time we met, Eden. Jealousy isn't an emotion I've been acquainted with in the past, and I'm afraid it's the only excuse I can offer.'

'Jealousy?' she repeated dizzily. Her thoughts were in a turmoil. She'd thought he had gone hurrying off to Adelaide, and here he was talking to *her* about jealousy. 'You were jealous—over me?'

'Murderously so,' he admitted grimly. 'You wouldn't know about it, Eden—you wouldn't understand how it can affect one's mind. Can you ever forgive me for the things I suspected?'

Eden, who in the past had so often had too much to say, was silent. They were in the open country, and Sin drove off the road into the trees by the river and presently pulled up. He got out of the car, came round and opened her door and she slipped out too, glancing at him quickly and giving him a pale smile. She felt wary, uncertain, yet, deep inside, terribly excited. They walked through the tree shadows till they stood in a quiet place from which they could see the brown waters of the river. A flock of galahs flew out of the trees and wheeled overhead, their underfeathers rose-coloured against the pallid sky of evening. The air was

189

hot and still, and a few cicadas burst into clamorous song and then were silent.

'You haven't said a word,' Sin said at last. She was standing with her back to a tree and he stood facing her, his hands against the broad tree trunk, one at either side of her shoulders. 'My nerves will snap in a minute. Are you going to look at me?'

He moved one hand and put a finger under her chin and turned her face up to his. Oh, God, had she ever thought he didn't have a kind face?—that his eyes were cold? She could die at this minute, just looking at him, and die happy. But she was thankful she didn't, because then he kissed her softly, lingeringly, only his lips touching her, until her whole body was melting and there were tears in her eyes.

'Bibi lied to me,' he said at last, drawing back from her, 'I know now.'

Eden nodded.

'And Berry Addison means nothing to you.' He stated it, he didn't ask, and she whispered, 'Nothing.' And then, because she couldn't help it, 'But—but *Christie*, Sin. I—I don't understand. Amy said you were in love with her—so why haven't you gone to Adelaide to persuade her? You could——'

He touched her lips. 'I've come to Kamballa to persuade you, Eden Dare,' he said quizzically. 'You're the one I'm in love with—but desperately. Don't you know that yet? Didn't I threaten to go to South America that day you flattened me with your cynicism at the *bora*? What was that all about? Christie again?'

She nodded, but didn't go into details. There were other more important things on her mind, such as whether she could believe what those green eyes of his seemed to be telling her—that Christie didn't matter, that Eden Dare was all-important. But was she? How could she be? Sin moved

190

to pull her into his arms, but she resisted.

'You were going to Bangkok with Christie. You only didn't go because of your work.'

He sighed and raised his eyebrows. 'You want to know everything, don't you? Very well, I'll be ungallant and tell you something, Eden. I was—briefly and superficially—in love with Christie. She has a very lovely face—but not half so lovely as yours!—and that, I'm afraid, sums her up as far as I'm concerned. Christie is—well, how shall I put it? Let's say that nature was niggardly in endowing her with sex instincts. She's more child than woman, she wants a father rather than a lover. Unfortunately, she made our love affair very public before it had ever begun.' He paused and grimaced slightly. 'I could have been brutal and just dropped her, but no one is unkind to Christie. I had to let her do the untangling herself—which she was glad enough to do after I administered a rather watered-down dose of passion, not at all to her taste! She'd insisted on coming to Bangkok, so I made my excuses at the last moment and let the girls go off on their own. It had the desired result, and I hope in Ralph she's picked a winner ... are you satisfied now, my darling?'

'Not quite,' said Eden after a moment. 'I was—I was jealous of Bibi too,' she admitted.

'Oh, forget Bibi,' he said dismissively and with distaste. 'I'm a male and she invited it. But she's a little vixen—she so nearly ruined everything.'

'What made you come, Sin? What made you—understand?'

'I had time to think after you'd gone. Too much time. And when Amy spoke up for you after I'd made some slighting remark about you of my ill-temper, the whole thing crystallised and I knew what a fool I'd been. Now, are you going to marry me? Or haven't I made out a good

191

enough case for myself?' He took hold of her two hands, and her eyes were held by his. 'Come here, Eden Dare,' he said indistinctly. 'I'll make one more effort to persuade you to say yes, and if it fails—I'll take you straight back to the Misses Martin.'

He drew her into his arms and his lips claimed hers demandingly, and her body was locked against his. It was all there—the thrill, the excitement, the danger. Love, she thought, was like the sea. It would carry her where it willed ...

When he let her go she said simply, 'Yes, Sin.'